MORE PRAISE FOR PAULA FOX'S

Desperate
Characters

"What gives this slice of life its timeless urgency is Fox's spare yet penetrating prose, shifting imperceptibly from present to past, external to internal, revealing the hushed despair, absurdity, and latent violence that lie beneath the most humdrum words and routines."
—**Charles Winecoff,** *Entertainment Weekly*

"As a writer, Fox is all sensitive, staring eyeball. Her images break the flesh. They scratch the retina. . . . Fox's prose hurts."
—**Walter Kirn,** *New York*

"*Desperate Characters*, with its bristling, hilarious dialogue and echoey, shadow-splashed silences, is a tour de force of ruthless compression. The glimpses of New York life at the peripheries of the Bentwoods' shrinking zone of safety are drawn unerringly, and suggest a view Dawn Powell might have provided if she'd lived to see the end of the sixties. . . . I treasure this book." —**Jonathan Lethem**

"Among the best things we have in contemporary literature—original, enduring, charged with intelligent, articulate life and with the tension of modern survival: brave, witty, alarming, and quite wonderful."
—**Shirley Hazzard**

"For all its brevity, its lack of side and posturing, *Desperate Characters* is a small masterpiece, a revelation . . . that grasps the mind of the reader with the subtle clarity of metaphor and the alarmed tenacity of nightmare. . . . It is an extraordinary achievement of passionate restraint and control." —**Pearl K. Bell,** *New Leader*

"Using a merciless camera's-eye style, Paula Fox . . . spreads problems before the reader and makes no recommendation. . . . The skillful insistency with which Miss Fox probes her characters' lives holds one's attention." **—Peter Rowley, *New York Times Book Review***

"One of the few novels I've quite literally kept near me over the years, to reread regularly. It's a model of profound and worldly insight and elegant style. . . . Paula Fox's beautifully calibrated sense of scale demonstrates the power of brevity and reticence. It's thrilling to see her book made available again." **—Rosellen Brown**

"Brilliant. . . . [Fox] is one of the most attractive writers to come our way in a long, long time." **—*The New Yorker***

"This perfect novel about pain is as clear, and as wholly believable, and as healing, as a fever dream." **—Frederick Busch**

"A piercing portrait of a modern couple at bay. . . . Relentlessly honest, brilliantly crafted, passionate." **—John Gabree, *New York Newsday***

"A brilliant performance, quite devastating in its mastery of the brutish New York scene." **—Alfred Kazin**

"A nearly perfect work, earning the reader's trust and respect from the very first sentence. . . . Fox shows us everything in a spare, beautifully crafted prose. . . . Every sentence yields pleasure—the pleasure of discovering a writer who knows the human heart. . . . *Desperate Characters* can be read and savored in one sitting." **—Diane Cole, *Georgia Review***

"A reserved and beautifully realized novel." **—Lionel Trilling**

"*Desperate Characters* takes its place in a major American tradition, the line of the short novel exemplified by *Billy Budd*, *The Great Gatsby*, *Miss Lonelyhearts*, and *Seize the Day*. . . . Grueling and brilliant."
—Irving Howe, *New Republic*

BOOKS BY PAULA FOX

Desperate Characters

PAULA FOX

Desperate
Characters

Introduction by Jonathan Franzen

 W. W. NORTON & COMPANY | NEW YORK · LONDON

Copyright © 1970 by Paula Fox

Introduction copyright © 1999 by Jonathan Franzen

Printed in the United States of America

First published as a Norton paperback 1999

Manufacturing by LSC Harrisonburg

Production Manager Louise Mattarelliano

The Library of Congress has cataloged an earlier edition as follows:

Fox, Paula.

    Desperate characters / Paula Fox: with an introduction by Jonathan Franzen.

          p.   cm.

    ISBN 0-393-31894-X (pbk.)

    I. Title.

PS3556.094D47   1999

813'.54—dc21

98-51183

ISBN 978-0-393-35110-1 pbk.

W. W. Norton & Company, Inc.

500 Fifth Avenue, New York, N.Y. 10110

www.wwnorton.com

W. W. Norton & Company Ltd.

15 Carlisle Street, London W1D 3BS

     7 8 9 0

No End to It:

Rereading *Desperate Characters*

On a first reading, *Desperate Characters* is a novel of suspense. Sophie Bentwood, a forty-year-old Brooklynite, is bitten by a stray cat to which she's given milk, and for the next three days she wonders what the bite is going to bring her: death of rabies? shots in the belly? nothing at all? The engine of the book is Sophie's cold-sweat dread. As in more conventional suspense novels, the stakes are life and death and, perhaps, the fate of the Free World. Sophie and her husband, Otto, are pioneering urban gentry in the late 1960s, when the civilization of the Free World's leading city seems to be crumbling under a barrage of garbage, vomit, and excrement, vandalism, fraud, and class hatred. Otto's longtime friend and law partner, Charlie Russel, quits the firm and attacks Otto savagely for his conservatism. Otto complains that a slovenly rural family's kitchen says "one thing" to him—it says *die*—and, indeed, this seems to be the message he gets from almost everything in his changing world. Sophie, for her part, wavers between dread and a strange wish to be harmed. She's terrified of a pain she's not sure she doesn't deserve. She clings to a world of privilege even as it suffocates her.

Along the way, page by page, are the pleasures of Paula Fox's prose. Her sentences are small miracles of compression and specificity, tiny novels in themselves. This is the moment of the cat bite:

> She smiled, wondering how often, if ever before, the cat had felt a friendly human touch, and she was still smiling as the cat reared up on its hind legs, even as it struck at her with extended claws, smiling right up to that second when it sank its teeth into the back of her left hand and hung from her flesh so that she nearly fell forward, stunned and horrified, yet conscious enough of Otto's presence to smother the cry that arose in her throat as she jerked her hand back from that circle of barbed wire.

By imagining a dramatic moment as a series of physical gestures—by paying close attention—Fox makes room here for each aspect of Sophie's complexity: her liberality, her self-delusion, her vulnerability, and, above all, her married-person's consciousness. *Desperate Characters* is the rare novel that does justice to both sides of marriage, both hate and love, both her and him. Otto is a man who loves his wife. Sophie is a woman who downs a shot of whiskey at six o'clock on a Monday morning and flushes out the kitchen sink "making loud childish sounds of disgust." Otto is mean enough to say, "Lotsa luck, fella" when Charlie leaves the firm; Sophie is mean enough to ask him, later, why he said

it; Otto is mortified when she does; Sophie is mortified for having mortified him.

The first time I read *Desperate Characters*, in 1991, I fell in
love with it. It seemed to me obviously superior to any novel by
Fox's contemporaries John Updike, Philip Roth, and Saul Bel-
low. It seemed inarguably great. And because I'd recognized
my own troubled marriage in the Bentwoods', and because
the novel had appeared to suggest that the fear of pain is more
destructive than pain itself, and because I wanted very much
to believe this, I reread it almost immediately. I hoped that the
book, on a second reading, might actually tell me how to live.

It did no such thing. It became, instead, more mysterious—
became less of a lesson and more of an experience. Previously
invisible metaphoric and thematic densities began to emerge.
My eye fell, for example, on a sentence describing dawn's arrival
in a living room: "Objects, their outlines beginning to harden
in the growing light, had a shadowy, totemic menace." In the
growing light of my second reading, I saw every object in the
book begin to harden in this way. Chicken livers, for example,
are introduced in the opening paragraph as a delicacy and as
the centerpiece of a cultivated dinner—as the essence of old-
world civilization. ("You take raw material and you transform
it," the leftist Leon remarks much later in the novel. "That *is*
civilization.") A day later, after the cat has bitten Sophie and she
and Otto have started fighting back, the leftover livers become
bait for the capture and killing of a wild animal. Cooked meat
is still the essence of civilization; but what a much more violent thing civilization now appears to be! Or follow the food in
another direction; see Sophie, shaken, on a Saturday morning,
trying to shore up her spirits by spending money on a piece of
cookware. She goes to the Bazaar Provençal to buy herself an

omelet pan, a prop for a "hazy domestic dream" of French ease and cultivation. The scene ends with the saleswoman throwing up her hands "as though to ward off a hex" and Sophie fleeing with a purchase almost comically emblematic of her desperation: an hourglass egg timer.

Although Sophie's hand is bleeding in this scene, her impulse is to deny it. The third time I read *Desperate Characters*—I'd assigned it in a fiction-writing class that I was teaching— I began to pay more attention to these denials. Sophie issues them more or less nonstop throughout the book: *It's all right. Oh, it's nothing. Oh, well, it's nothing. Don't talk to me about it. THE CAT WASN'T SICK! It's a bite, just a bite! I won't go running off to the hospital for something as foolish as this. It's nothing. It's much better. It's of no consequence.* These repeated denials mirror the underlying structure of the novel: Sophie flees from one potential haven to another, and each in turn fails to protect her. She goes to a party with Otto, she sneaks out with Charlie, she buys herself a present, she seeks comfort in old friends, she reaches out to Charlie's wife, she tries to phone her old lover, she agrees to go to the hospital, she catches the cat, she takes to bed, she tries to read a French novel, she flees to her beloved country house, she thinks about moving to another time zone, she thinks about adopting children, she destroys an old friendship: nothing brings relief. Her last hope is to write to her mother about the cat bite, to "strike the exact note calculated to arouse the old woman's scorn and hilarity"—to make her plight into art, in other words. But Otto throws her ink bottle at the wall.

What is Sophie running from? The fourth time I read *Desperate Characters*, I hoped I'd get an answer. I wanted to figure out, finally, whether it's a happy thing or a terrible thing that the Bentwoods' life breaks open on the last page of the book. I wanted to "get" the final scene. But I still didn't get it. I consoled myself with the idea that good fiction is defined, in large part, by its refusal to offer the easy answers of ideology, the cures of a therapeutic culture, or the pleasantly resolving dreams of mass entertainment. Maybe *Desperate Characters* wasn't so much about answers as about the persistence of questions. I was struck by Sophie's resemblance to Hamlet—another morbidly self-conscious character who receives a disturbing and ambiguous message, undergoes torments while trying to decide what the message means, and finally puts himself in the hands of a providential "divinity" and accepts his fate. For Sophie Bentwood, the ambiguous message comes not from a ghost but from a cat bite, and her agony is less about uncertainty than about an *unwillingness* to face the truth. Near the end, when she addresses a divinity and says, *"God, if I am rabid, I am equal to what is outside,"* it's not a moment of revelation. It's a moment of relief.

A BOOK THAT has fallen even briefly out of print can put a strain on the most devoted reader's love. In the way that a man might regret certain shy mannerisms in his wife that cloud her beauty, or a woman might wish that her husband laughed less loudly at his own jokes, though the jokes are very funny, I've suffered for the tiny imperfections that might prejudice potential readers against *Desperate Characters*. I'm thinking of the stiffness and impersonality of the opening paragraph, the austerity of the opening sentence, the creaky word "repast." As a lover of the book, I now appreciate how the formality and stasis of this paragraph set up the short, sharp line of dialogue that follows ("The cat is back"), but what if a reader never makes it past "repast"? I wonder, too, if the name "Otto Bentwood" might be difficult to take on first reading. Fox generally works her characters' names very hard—the name "Russel," for instance, nicely echoes Charlie's restless, furtive energies (Otto suspects him of "rustling" clients), and just as something is surely missing in Charlie's character, a second "l" is missing in his surname. I do admire how the old-fashioned and vaguely Teutonic name "Otto" saddles Otto, much as his own compulsive orderliness saddles him; but "Bentwood," even after many readings, remains for me a little artificial in its bonsai imagery. And then there's the title of the book. It's apt, certainly, and yet it's no *The Day of the Locust*, no *The Great Gatsby*, no *Absalom, Absalom!* It's a title that people may forget or confuse with other titles. Sometimes, wishing it were stronger, I feel lonely in the peculiar way of someone deeply married.

As the years have gone by, I've continued to dip in and out of *Desperate Characters*, seeking comfort or reassurance from passages of familiar beauty. Now, though, as I reread the book in its entirety, I'm amazed by how much of it is still fresh and unfamiliar to me. I never paid attention, for example, to Otto's anecdote, late in the book, about Cynthia Kornfeld and her husband the anarchist artist. I'd never noticed how Cynthia Kornfeld's jello-and-nickels salad mocks the Bentwood equation of food and privilege and civilization, or how the notion of typewriters retrofitted to spew nonsense prefigures the novel's closing image, or how the anecdote insists that *Desperate Characters* be read in the context of a contemporary art scene whose aim is the destruction of order and meaning. And Charlie Russel— have I ever really *seen* him until now? In my earlier readings he remained a kind of stock villain, a turncoat, an egregious man. Now he seems to me almost as important to the story as the cat. He's Otto's only friend; his phone call precipitates the final crisis; he produces the Thoreau quotation that gives the book its title; and he delivers a verdict on the Bentwoods—"drearily enslaved by introspection while the foundation of their privilege is being blasted out from under them"—that feels ominously dead-on.

At this late date, however, I'm not sure I even want fresh insights. As Sophie and Otto suffer from too-intimate knowledge of each other, I now suffer from too-intimate knowledge of *Desperate Characters*. My underlining and marginal annotations are getting out of hand. In my latest reading, I'm finding and flagging as vital and central an enormous number of previously unflagged images involving order and chaos and childhood and adulthood. Because the book is not long, and because I've now read it half a dozen times, I'm within sight of the point at which *every sentence* will be highlighted as vital and central. This extraordinary richness is, of course, a testament to Paula Fox's genius. There's hardly an extraneous or arbitrary word to be found in the book. Rigor and thematic density of such magnitude don't happen by accident, and yet it's almost impossible for a writer to achieve them while relaxing enough to allow the characters to come alive, and yet here the novel is, soaring above every other work of American realist fiction since the Second World War.

The irony of the novel's richness, however, is that the better I grasp the import of each individual sentence, the less able I am to articulate what grand, global meaning all these local meanings might be serving. There's finally a kind of horror to an overload of meaning. It's closely akin, as Melville suggests in "The Whiteness of the Whale" in *Moby-Dick*, to a total whiteout *absence* of meaning. The tracking and deciphering and organizing of life's significance can swamp the actual living of it, and in *Desperate Characters* the reader is not the only one who's swamped. The Bentwoods themselves are highly literate, thoroughly modern creatures. Their curse is that they're all too well equipped to read themselves as literary texts dense with overlapping meanings. In the course of one late-winter weekend, they become oppressed and finally overwhelmed by the way in which the most casual words and tiniest incidents feel like "portents." The enormous suspense the book develops is not just a product of Sophie's dread, then, or of Fox's step-by-step closing of every possible avenue of escape, or of her equation of a crisis in a marital partnership with a crisis in a business partnership and a crisis in American urban life. More than anything else, it's the slow cresting of a crushingly heavy wave of literary significance. Sophie consciously and explicitly invokes rabies as a metaphor for her emotional and political plight, and even as Otto breaks down and cries out about how desperate he is, he cannot avoid "quoting" (in the postmodern sense) his and Sophie's earlier conversation about Thoreau, thereby invoking all the other themes and dialogues threading through the weekend, in particular Charlie's vexing of the issue of "desperation." As bad as it is to be desperate, it's even worse to be desperate and also be aware of the vital questions of public law and order and privilege and Thoreauvian interpretation that are entailed in your private desperation, and to feel as if by breaking down you're proving a whole nation of Charlie Russels right. When Sophie declares her wish to be rabid, as when Otto hurls the ink bottle, both seem to be revolting against an unbearable, almost murderous sense of the *importance* of their words and thoughts. Small wonder that the last actions of the book are wordless—that Sophie and Otto have "ceased to listen" to the words streaming from the telephone, and that the thing written in ink which they turn slowly to read is a violent, wordless blot. No sooner has Fox achieved the most dazzling success at finding order in the nonevents of one late-winter weekend than, with the perfect gesture, she repudiates that order.

Desperate Characters is a novel in revolt against its own perfection. The questions it raises are radical and unpleasant. What is the point of meaning—especially literary meaning—in a rabid modern world? Why bother creating and preserving order if civilization is every bit as killing as the anarchy to which it's opposed? Why not be rabid? Why torment ourselves with books? Rereading the novel for the sixth or seventh time, I feel a cresting rage and frustration with its mysteries and with the paradoxes of civilization and with the insufficiency of my own brain and then, as if out of nowhere, I *do* get the ending—I feel what Otto Bentwood feels when he smashes the ink bottle against the wall—and suddenly I'm in love all over again.

Jonathan Franzen

January 1999

Desperate
Characters

ONE

Mr. and Mrs. Otto Bentwood drew out their chairs simultaneously. As he sat down, Otto regarded the straw basket which held slices of French bread, an earthenware casserole filled with sautéed chicken livers, peeled and sliced tomatoes on an oval willowware platter Sophie had found in a Brooklyn Heights antique shop, and *risotto* Milanese in a green ceramic bowl. A strong light, somewhat softened by the stained glass of a Tiffany shade, fell upon this repast. A few feet away from the dining room table, an oblong of white, the reflection from a fluorescent tube over a stainless-steel sink, lay upon the floor in front of the entrance to the kitchen. The old sliding doors that had once separated the two first-floor rooms had long since been removed, so that by turning slightly the Bentwoods could glance down the length of their living room where, at this hour, a standing lamp with a shade like half a white sphere was always lit, and they could, if they chose, view the old cedar planks of the floor, a bookcase which held, among other volumes, the complete works of Goethe and two shelves of French poets, and the highly polished corner of a Victorian secretary.

Otto unfolded a large linen napkin with deliberation.

"The cat is back," said Sophie.

"Are you surprised?" Otto asked. "What did you expect?"

Sophie looked beyond Otto's shoulder at the glass door that opened onto a small wooden stoop, suspended above the back yard like a crow's nest. The cat was rubbing its scruffy, half-starved body against the base of the door with soft insistence. Its gray fur, the gray of tree fungus, was faintly striped. Its head was massive, a pumpkin, jowled and unprincipled and grotesque.

"Stop watching it," Otto said. "You shouldn't have fed it in the first place."

"I suppose."

"We'll have to call the A.S.P.C.A."

"Poor thing."

"It does very well for itself. All those cats do well."

"Perhaps their survival depends on people like me."

"These livers are good," he said. "I don't see that it matters whether they survive or not."

The cat flung itself against the door.

"Ignore it," Otto said. "Do you want all the wild cats in Brooklyn holding a food vigil on our porch? Think what they do to the garden! I saw one catch a bird the other day. They're not pussycats, you know. They're thugs."

"Look how late the light stays now!"

"The days are getting longer. I hope the locals don't start up with their goddamn bongos. Perhaps it will rain the way it did last spring."

"Will you want coffee?"

"Tea. The rain locks them in."

"The rain's not on your *side*, Otto!"

He smiled. "Yes, it is."

She did not smile at him. When she went to the kitchen, Otto quickly turned toward the door. The cat, at that instant, rammed its head against the glass. "Ugly bastard!" Otto muttered. The cat looked at him, then its eyes flicked away. The house felt powerfully solid to him; the sense of that solidity was like a hand placed firmly in the small of his back. Across the yard, past the cat's agitated movements, he saw the rear windows of the houses on the slum street. Some windows had rags tacked across them, others, sheets of transparent plastic. From the sill of one, a blue blanket dangled. There was a long tear in the middle of it through which he could see the faded pink brick of the wall. The tattered end of the blanket just touched the top frame of a door which, as Otto was about to turn away, opened. A fat elderly woman in a bathrobe shouldered her way out into the yard and emptied a large paper sack over the ground. She stared down at the garbage for a moment, then shuffled back inside. Sophie returned with cups and saucers.

"I met Bullin on the street," Otto said. "He told me two more houses have been sold over there." He gestured toward the rear windows with his hand. Out of the corner of his eye, he saw the cat leap as though he had offered it something.

"What happens to the people in them when the houses are bought? Where do they go? I always wonder about that."

"I don't know. Too many people everywhere."

"Who bought the houses?"

"A brave pioneer from Wall Street. And the other, I think, a painter who got evicted from his loft on Lower Broadway."

"It doesn't take courage. It takes cash."

"The rice is wonderful, Sophie."

"Look! He's curled up on that little ledge. How can he fit himself into such a small space?"

"They're like snakes."

"Otto, I'll just give him a little milk. I know I shouldn't have fed him in the first place. But he's here now. We'll be going out to Flynders in June. By the time we come home, he'll have found someone else."

"Why do you persist? It's self-indulgence. Look! You don't mind at all as long as you don't have to *see* the cat looking starved. That goddamn woman just dumped her evening load of garbage over there. Why doesn't the cat go there to eat?"

"I don't care why I'm doing it," Sophie said. "The point is that I *can* see it starving."

"What time are we due at the Holsteins?"

"Nine-ish," she said, on her way to the door with a saucer of milk. She reached up and inserted a small key in the lock, which had been placed on a crosspiece above the frame. Then she turned the brass handle.

At once the cat cried out, and began to lap up the milk. From other houses came the faint rattle of plates and pots, the mumble of television sets and radios—but the sheer multiplicity of noises made it difficult to identify individual ones.

The cat's huge head hung over the little Meissen saucer. Sophie stooped and drew her hand along its back, which quivered beneath her fingers.

"Come back in and shut the door!" Otto complained. "It's getting cold in here."

A dog's anguished yelp broke suddenly through the surface of the evening hum.

"My God!" exclaimed Otto. "What are they doing to that animal!"

"Catholics believe that animals have no souls," Sophie said.

"Those people aren't Catholics. What are you talking about! They all go to that Pentecostal *iglesia* up the street."

The cat had begun to clean its whiskers. Sophie caressed its back again, drawing her fingers along until they met the sharp furry crook where the tail turned up. The cat's back rose convulsively to press against her hand. She smiled, wondering how often, if ever before, the cat had felt a friendly human touch, and she was still smiling as the cat reared up on its hind legs, even as it struck at her with extended claws, smiling right up to that second when it sank its teeth into the back of her left hand and hung from her flesh so that she nearly fell forward, stunned and horrified, yet conscious enough of Otto's presence to smother the cry that arose in her throat as she jerked her hand back from that circle of barbed wire. She pushed out with her other hand, and as the sweat broke out on her forehead, as her flesh crawled and tightened, she said, "No, no, stop that!" to the cat, as though it had done nothing more than beg for food, and in the midst of her pain and dismay she was astonished to hear how cool her voice was. Then, all at once, the claws released her and flew back as though to deliver another blow, but then the cat turned—it seemed in mid-air—and sprang from the porch, disappearing into the shadowed yard below.

"Sophie? What happened?"

"Nothing," she said. "I'm going to get the tea now." She pushed the door closed and walked quickly to the kitchen, keeping her back turned to Otto. Her heart pounded. She tried to

breathe deeply to subdue that noisy thud and she wondered
fleetingly at the shame she felt—as though she'd been caught
in some despicable act.

Standing at the kitchen sink, clenching her hands, she told
herself it was nothing. A long scratch at the base of her thumb
bled slowly, but blood gushed from the bite. She turned on the
water. Her hands looked drained; the small frecklelike blotches
which had begun to appear during the winter were livid. She
leaned forward against the sink, wondering if she were going
to faint. Then she washed her hands with yellow kitchen soap.
She licked her skin, tasting soap and blood, then covered the
bite with a scrap of paper toweling.

When she returned with the tea, Otto was looking through
some legal papers bound in blue covers. He glanced up at her,
and she looked back at him with apparent calm, then placed his
tea in front of him with her right hand, keeping the other out of
sight at her side. Still, he seemed faintly puzzled, as though he'd
heard a sound he couldn't identify. She forestalled any questions
by asking him at once if he'd like some fruit. He said no, and the
moment passed.

"You left the door open. You have to lock it, Sophie, or it just
swings back."

She closed the door again, securing it with the key. Through
the glass, she saw the saucer. Already there were a few spots of
soot in it. She'd given up cigarettes in the fall, but it didn't seem
much use. I can't unlock the door again, she said to herself.

"It's done," Otto said. He sighed. "Done, at last."

"What's done?"

"Deaf Sophie. You really don't listen to me any more. Charlie moved out today, to his new office. He didn't even tell me
until this morning that he'd actually found a place. He said he

wanted the whole thing to be a clean break. 'If I need the files, can I get in touch with you?' That's what he asked me. Even in such a question, he implies that I'm likely to be unreasonable."

She sat down, keeping her left hand on her lap.

"You've never said much about any of it to me," she said.

"There wasn't much to say. In this last year we haven't agreed on anything, not anything. If I said it was going to rain, Charlie would pull at his lower lip and say, no, it wasn't going to rain. After reading the weather reports carefully, he judged it was going to be a fine clear day. I should have learned a long time ago that character doesn't change. I made all the superficial adjustments I could."

"You've been together such a long time. Why have you come to this now?"

"I don't care for the new people he's taken up with, the clients. I know what's always gone on in the office. I've done the tiresome work while Charlie's put on his funny hats and knocked everybody dead with personal charm. His whole act has consisted in denying the law is anything but an ironic joke, and that goes far with a lot of people."

"It will be hard to see them. Don't you think it will? Ruth and I've never been close friends, but we managed. How do you just stop seeing people? What about the boat?"

"You just stop, that's how. The winter has been so bad. You can't imagine the people in the waiting room, a beggar's army. He told me today that some of his clients were intimidated by the grandeur of our office, that they'll be more comfortable in year before his new place. Then he said I'd dry up and disappear if I didn't, in his words, tune in on the world. God! You should hear him talk, as though he'd been sanctified! One of his clients accused the receptionist of being racist because she asked him to use an ashtray instead of grinding his cigarette butt out in the rug. And today, two men like comic-strip spies helped him pack his goddamn cartons. No, we won't be seeing them and he can have the boat. I've never cared that much about it. Really, it's just been a burden."

Sophie winced as she felt a thrust of sharp pain. He frowned at her and she saw that he thought she hadn't liked what he had said. She'd tell him now, might as well. The incident with the cat was silly. At a distance of half an hour, she wondered at the terror she'd felt, and the shame.

"The cat scratched me," she said. He got up at once and walked around the table to her.

"Let me see."

She held up her hand. It was hurting. He touched it delicately, and his face showed solicitude. It flashed through her mind that he was sympathetic because the cat had justified his warning against it.

"Did you wash it? Did you put something on it?"

"Yes, yes," she answered impatiently, watching the blood seep through the paper, thinking to herself that if the bleeding would stop, that would be an end to it.

"Well, I'm sorry, darling. But it wasn't a good idea to feed it."

"No. It wasn't."

"Does it hurt?"

"A little. Like an insect bite."

"Just take it easy for a while. Read the paper."

He cleared the table, put the dishes in the dishwasher, scraped the remaining livers into a bowl and set the casserole to soak. As he went about his work, he caught glimpses of Sophie, sitting up very straight, the newspaper on her lap. He was curiously touched by her uncharacteristic immobility. She appeared to be listening for something, waiting.

Sophie sat in the living room and stared at the front page of the newspaper. Her hand had begun to throb. It was only her hand, she told herself, yet the rest of her body seemed involved in a way she couldn't understand. It was as though she'd been vitally wounded.

Otto walked into the living room. "What are you going to wear?" he asked her cheerfully.

"That Pucci dress," she said, "although I think I've put on too much weight for it." She got up. "Otto, why did it bite me? I was petting it."

"I thought you said it just scratched you."

"Whatever it did . . . but why did it attack me so?" They walked to the staircase. The mahogany banister glowed in the soft buttery light of a Victorian bubble-glass globe which hung from the ceiling. She and Otto had worked for a week taking off the old black paint from the banister. It was the first thing they had done together after they had bought the house.

"Because it's savage," he said. "Because all it wanted from you was food." He put his foot on the first step and said, as if to himself, "I'll be better off by myself."

"You've always had your own clients," she said irritably, clenching and unclenching her hurt hand. "I don't see why you couldn't keep on together."

"All that melodrama . . . I can't live with that. And he couldn't leave it alone. If I wasn't with him, I was against him. I don't mean to say there isn't cause. I don't mean to say there's any kind of justice in the world. But I know Charlie. He's using those people and their causes. He just doesn't want to be left out.

And I *want* to be left out. Oh . . . it was time it all ended. We've used each other up. The truth is, I don't like him any more."

"I wonder how he feels?"

"Like Paul Muni, defending the unlovely and unloved. There never were such lawyers. Do you remember? All those movies in the thirties? The young doctors and lawyers going to the sticks and edifying all the rubes?"

"Paul Muni! Charlie's right," she said. "You're barely in the right century."

"That's true."

"But Charlie is not *bad!*" she exclaimed.

"I didn't say he was bad. He's irresponsible and vain and hysterical. Bad hasn't anything to do with it."

"Irresponsible! What do you mean, irresponsible!"

"Shut up!" said Otto. He put his arms around her.

"Look out!" she said. "I'll get blood on you!"

TWO

A few feet from the bottom step, Otto paused and turned, as he habitually did, to look back at his home. He was drawn toward it. He yearned to throw open the door he had only just locked, to *catch* the house empty. It was, he thought, a little like the wish to be sentient at one's own funeral.

With one or two exceptions, each of the houses on the Bentwoods' block was occupied by one family. All of the houses had been built during the final third of the last century, and were of brick or brownstone. Where the brick had been cleaned, a chalky pink glow gave off an air of antique serenity. Most front parlor windows were covered with white shutters. Where owners had not yet been able to afford them, pieces of fabric concealed the life within behind the new panes of glass. These bits of cloth, even though they were temporary measures, had a certain style, a kind of forethought about taste, and were not at all like the rags that hung over the windows of the slum people. What the owners of the street lusted after was recognition of their superior comprehension of what counted in this world, and their strategy for getting it combined restraint and indirection.

One boardinghouse remained in business, but the nine tenants were very quiet, almost furtive, like the last remaining members of a foreign enclave who, daily, expect deportation.

The neighborhood eyesore was a house covered with yellow tile. An Italian family that had lived on the block during its worst days, finally moving out the day after all the street lamps had been smashed, was held responsible for this breach of taste.

The maple trees planted by the neighborhood association the year before were beginning to bud. But the street was not well lighted yet, and despite phone calls, letters, and petitions to City Hall and the local precinct, policemen were rarely glimpsed, except in patrol cars on their way to the slum people. At night, the street had a quiet earnest look, as though it were continuing to try to improve itself in the dark.

There was still refuse everywhere, a tide that rose but barely ebbed. Beer bottles and beer cans, liquor bottles, candy wrappers, crushed cigarette packs, caved-in boxes that had held detergents, rags, newspapers, curlers, string, plastic bottles, a shoe here and there, dog feces. Otto had once said, staring disgustedly at the curb in front of their house, that no dog had deposited *that*.

"Do you suppose they come here to shit at night?" he had asked Sophie.

She hadn't replied, only giving him a sidelong glance that was touched with amusement. What would he have said, she wondered, if she had told him that his question had reminded her of a certain period in her childhood when moving the bowels, as her mother called it, was taken up by Sophie and her friends as an outdoor activity, until they were all caught in a community squat beneath a lilac bush? Sophie had been shut into the bathroom for an hour, in order, her mother had said, to study the proper receptacle for such functions.

The Holsteins lived in Brooklyn Heights on Henry Street, ten blocks from the Bentwoods. Otto didn't want to take the car and lose his parking space, and although Sophie did not feel up to walking—she was vaguely nauseated—she didn't want to insist on being driven. Otto would think the cat bite had affected her more than it really had. It was usually more costly to make a fool of oneself, she thought. Her fatuity had deserved at least a small puncture.

"*Why* do they drop everything on the pavement?" Otto asked angrily.

"It's the packaging. Wrapping frenzy."

"It's simple provocation. I watched a colored man kick over a trash basket yesterday. When it rolled out into the street, he put his hands on his hips and roared with laughter. This morning I saw that man who hangs the blanket outside his window standing on his bed and pissing out into the yard."

A car in low gear passed; a window slid down and a hand gently released a ball of Kleenex. Sophie began to laugh. "Americans . . ." muttered Otto, "softly dropping their turds wherever they go."

They crossed Atlantic Avenue and started west, passing the Arab shops with their windows full of leather cushions and hookahs, the Arab bakeries which smelled of sesame paste. A thin Eastern wail slid out of a store no bigger than a closet. Inside, three men were staring down at a hand-operated record player. Sophie paused in front of a Jordanian restaurant, where the Bentwoods had dined with Charlie Russel and his wife only last week. Looking past the flaking gold letters on the glass, she saw the table they had sat at.

"How is it possible? It all seemed so friendly that night," she said softly.

"It was. When we first decided to end the partnership, it was friendlier than it ever had been. But this week . . ."

"It's not that you ever agreed on anything—but it all seemed so set."

"No, we didn't agree."

She exclaimed suddenly and held up her hand.

"What is it?" he asked.

"You brushed against it."

They stopped beneath a light while Otto inspected her hand.

"It's swollen," he said. "Looks awful."

"It's all right, just sensitive."

The bleeding had stopped, but a small lump had formed, pushing up the lips of the wound.

"I think you ought to see a doctor. You ought, at least, to get a tetanus shot."

"What do you mean, 'at least'?" she cried irritably.

"Don't be so bad-tempered."

They turned up Henry Street. Otto noted with satisfaction that there was as much garbage here as in their own neighborhood. He wouldn't consider buying a house on the Heights . . . horribly inflated prices, all that real-estate grinning in dusty crumbling rooms—think what you could do with that woodwork!—everyone knowing it was a put-up job, greed, low belly greed, get it while we can, house prices enunciated in refined accents, mortgages like progressive diseases, "I live on the Heights." Of course, the Bentwoods' neighborhood was on the same ladder, frantic lest the speculators now eying property were the "wrong" kind. Otto hated realtors, hated dealing with their nasty litigations. It was the only thing he and Charlie still agreed on. He sighed, thinking of the cop who had been checking on voter registration last week, who had said to Otto, "This area is really pulling itself together, doesn't look like the same place it was two years ago. You people are doing a job!" And Otto had felt a murderous gratification.

"What are you sighing about?" Sophie asked.

"I don't know."

The Bentwoods had a high income. They had no children and, since they were both just over forty (Sophie was two months older than Otto), they didn't anticipate any. They could purchase pretty much what they wanted. They had a Mercedes-Benz sedan and a house on Long Island with a long-term mortgage, which was hardly a burden any more. It sat in a meadow near the village of Flynders. Like their Brooklyn house, it was small, but it was a century older. Otto had paid for repairs out of cash reserves. In the seven years they had owned it, there had been only one disagreeable summer. That was when three homosexual men had rented a neighboring barn and played Judy Garland records all night long every night. They had set their portable record player on a cement birdbath in the old cow pasture. In moonlight or in fog, Judy Garland's voice rang out across the meadow, driving into Otto's head like a mailed fist. That September, he bought the barn. Someday he planned to convert it into a guest house. At present it housed the sailboat he shared with Russel.

"I think I'll just give the boat to Charlie," he said as they walked up the steps to the Holsteins' door. "I don't even remember how much money we each put in."

"Where's he going to sail it?" Sophie asked. "In the Bowery?"

The goddamn bite had made her nervous, he thought, and when she was nervous the quality he valued in her most—her equableness—disappeared. She seemed almost to narrow physically. He pressed the bell beneath the severe black plate on which was printed MYRON HOLSTEIN, M.D. Even if he was a psychoanalyst, he ought to know something about animal bites, Otto told her, but Sophie said she didn't want to make an issue of it. It already felt better. "Please don't bring it up. Just that I would like to leave early—" Then the door opened.

There were so many people wandering around beneath Flo Holstein's brilliant wall lights that it looked as if a sale were in progress. Even at a glance, Sophie saw some among the multitude who were strangers to the house. These few were looking covertly at furniture and paintings. There wasn't a copy of anything on the premises. It was real Miës van der Rohe, real Queen Anne, real Matisse and Gottlieb.

Flo had produced two successful musicals. Mike Holstein's practice was largely made up of writers and painters. Sophie liked him. Otto said he suffered from culture desperation. "He can't stand his own trade," Otto had said. "He's like one of those movie starlets who announces she's studying philosophy at U.C.L.A."

But at that moment Sophie—her face held in Dr. Holstein's strong square hands—felt the nervous tension of the last two hours draining out of her as though she'd been given a mild soporific.

"Soph, darling! Hello, Otto. Sophie, you look marvelous! Is that dress a Pucci? What a relief that you don't fiddle with your hair. That style makes you look like some sad lovely girl out of the thirties. Did you know that?" He kissed her in the manner of other people's husbands, on the cheek, dry-lipped and ritualistic.

He didn't know a thing about her, not even after ten years, but she loved the air of knowingness; the flattery that didn't obligate her. And she liked his somewhat battered face, the close-fitting English suits he bought from a London salesman who stopped at a mid-town hotel each year to take orders, the Italian shoes he said were part of his seducer's costume. He wasn't a seducer. He was remote. He was like a man preceded into a room by acrobats.

Despite her resolve to say nothing, she found herself whispering into his neck. "Something awful happened . . . I'm making too much of it, I know, but it was awful. . . ."

As he led her toward the kitchen, a man grabbed Otto's arm, shouted something, and dragged him into a group near the fireplace. In the kitchen, Flo kissed her hurriedly and turned to look at a huge orange casserole squatting inside the face-level wall oven. Two men, one of them turning the water tap off and on and staring pensively in the sink, did not look up.

"What happened? Do you want your gin on the rocks?" Mike asked.

"A cat bit me."

"Let's see."

She held up her hand. The slack fingers looked somewhat pitiful, she thought. Since she and Otto had looked at it under the street lamp, the bump appeared to have grown larger. It was tinged with yellow.

"Listen, that ought to be looked at!"

"Oh, it's nothing. I've been bitten before by animals." But she hadn't. "It was a shock," she said, stammering slightly as if she'd tripped over her lie, "because I'd been feeding the damned beast and it turned on me."

"I don't think there's been any rabies around here in years, but—"

"No," she said. "No, not a chance. That cat was perfectly healthy. You know me. I want to be the saint who tames wild creatures."

"Mike!" Flo cried. "Get the door, will you? Here, what are you drinking, Sophie?"

"Nothing right now," Sophie answered. Mike left her with a pat on the back, a nod that said he'd return. One of the young men began to comb his hair. Sophie went into the long living room. A television comedian she had met before at the Holsteins' was holding forth among a group of seated people, none of whom was paying him much attention. In a voice of maniacal self-confidence, he reported that since he'd grown his beard, he couldn't eat cooked cereal any more without making a swine of himself. When no one laughed, he caressed the growth at his chin and on his cheeks. "No kidding!" he cried. "These kids nowadays are wunnerful! Hair is for real! I wanna live and love and be myself. That's the message! Seriously." He was short and pudgy and his skin glistened like lard.

"A very Gentile party," someone said over Sophie's shoulder. She turned and saw a couple in their early twenties. The girl was in a white leather suit; the boy wore an army fatigue jacket, on which were pinned buttons shaped and painted like eyeballs, staring from nothing, at nothing. His frizzy hair shot off in all directions like a pubic St. Catherine's wheel. The girl was beautiful—young and unmarked. Her amber hair fell to her waist. She wore a heavy bracelet around one of her ankles.

"I saw at least three Jews," Sophie said.

They didn't smile. "Your parties are educational," the girl said. "It isn't my party," Sophie replied.

"Yes, it's yours," the boy said judiciously. "Your generation's thing."

"Oh, for crissakes!" Sophie said, smiling.

They looked at each other. The boy touched the girl's hair. "She's a wicked one, isn't she?" The girl nodded slowly.

"You must be young Mike's friends?" asked Sophie. Young Mike was lurching through C.C.N.Y. but each semester's end brought terror into the Holstein household. Would he go back once more?

"Let's split," said the boy. "We've got to go see Lonnie up in St. Luke's."

"The hospital?" asked Sophie. "It's too late for visiting hours."

They looked at her as though they'd never seen her before, then they both padded softly out of the living room, looking neither left nor right. "That's a beautiful anklet!" Sophie called out. The girl looked back from the hall. For an instant, she seemed about to smile. "It hurts me to wear it," she shouted. "Every time I move, it hurts."

Otto was backed up against a wall, looking up at the chin of a powerfully built woman wearing pants and jacket. She was an English playwright, a friend of Flo's, who wrote exclusively in verse. Otto, Sophie observed as she walked over to them, had one hand behind him pressed against the wooden paneling.

"We are all of us dying of boredom," the woman was saying. "That is the why of the war, the why of the assassinations, the why of why. Boredom."

"The younger ones are dying of freedom," Otto said in a voice flattened by restraint. Sophie caught his eye. He shook his head very slightly.

"The young will save us," the woman said. "It's the young, thank the dead God, who will save us."

"They are dying from what they are trying to cure themselves with," Otto said.

"You *are* a square!" the woman said, stooping a little to look into his face.

"Hello, Suzanne," Sophie said. "I just heard someone say, 'I'm crashing.' What does it mean?" She realized she had a fake ingenuous look on her face. It was obscurely insulting and she hoped Suzanne would feel the edge.

"In contemporary parlance," Suzanne explained magnanimously, "it means either that you've come to spend the night in someone's pad, or that you are coming down from a drug high." She bowed to Otto and moved away. She rarely spoke to men when other women were around.

"Jesus!" Otto exclaimed. "Trying to stop her from talking is like trying to get a newspaper under a dog before it pukes!"

"I hate it when you talk like that! You're getting worse as you get older. I can't bear that mean reductive—"

"Where's your drink?"

"I don't want a drink," she said irritably. He stood directly in front of her, blocking out the room. There was hesitancy in his look. He had heard her, hearing him, and he was sorry. She could see that, sorry herself now that she had spoken so meanly. For a second, they held each other's gaze. "That button's loose," she said, touching his jacket. "I'll get you something . . ." he said, but he didn't move away. They had averted what was ordinary; they had felt briefly the force of something original, unknown, between them. Even as she tried to name it, it was dissolving, and he left her suddenly just as she had forgotten what she was trying to remember. She flattened her hand against the wall

paneling. It looked like a tarantula. Her skin prickled. Rabies
. . . no one ever got rabies, except some Southern country boy.

"Sophie, come here," Mike said, and led her upstairs and
into a large bedroom. A Greek rug covered the bed; a Mexican
ceramic horse stood in front of the fireplace. On one of the bedside tables were piled paperback detective stories in their penny
candy wrapper covers.

"Who reads those? You or Flo?"

"Me," he replied, and he sighed and looked winsome.
"They're good for me. They ride roughshod over what I live
with. Potent men. Palpitating women . . . a murderer's mind
laid out like the contents of a child's pencil box."

"You aren't reading the right ones."

"The new ones are the old ones. That false complexity is just
another kind of pencil box."

"What's going to happen?" she burst out. "Everything is
going to hell—"

"Sit down a minute and shut up! I want to call a doctor or
two, see if I can rouse one. It's a bad night for that."

He sat on the edge of the bed and dialed, an address book
held tightly in one hand, the phone cradled between his neck
and shoulder. She heard him speak several times, but she didn't
listen to his words. She was wandering around the room. A
green silk dressing gown was flung across a chaise lounge. On
the mantelpiece stood a few small pre-Columbian statues, glar-
ing with empty malevolence at the opposite wall, looking, oddly
enough, as though they were outside the room but about to enter
and sack it.

"There are only answering services," Mike said, putting the
phone down. "There's not much point in leaving this number.
Listen, I want you to go to the hospital. It's six blocks from here

and they have an emergency room that's not bad. They'll fix you up and you'll have a peaceful night."

"Did you know?" she began, "that Cervantes wanted to come to the New World, to New Spain, and the king wrote across his application, 'No, tell him to get a job around here'? Isn't that a funny story?"

He watched her, unmoving, his hands folded lightly, his shoulders hunched—it must be the way he listened to patients, she thought, as though he were about to receive a blow across the back.

"Just a story . . ."

"What's the matter?"

"I wish I were Jewish," she said. "Then when I died, I'd die as a Jew."

"You'll die as a Protestant."

"There aren't many left."

"Then as a Gentile. I asked you, what's the matter? Are you working on anything?"

"I haven't wanted to work; it seems futile. There are so many who do it better than I do. I was sent a novel to translate but I couldn't understand it, even in French. It simply irritated me. And I don't *have* to work."

"Tell me a little Baudelaire," he said.

"Je suis comme le roi d'un pays pluvieux,
Riche, mais impuissant, jeune et pourtant très vieux—"

She broke off, laughing. "Why, you love it! You should see your face! Wait! Here!" and she snatched up a hand mirror from the top of a bureau and held it in front of him. He looked at her over the mirror. "I could smack you," he said.

"No, no . . . you don't understand. I like the way you looked. That I could just recite a few lines and evoke that look!"

"Helpless bliss," he said, getting to his feet.

"You know that Charlie and Otto are ending their partnership?"

"Otto doesn't confide in me."

"They can't get along any more," she said, replacing the mirror and turning back to him. "It'll change our life, and yet it is as though nothing has happened."

"It won't change your life," he said with a touch of impatience. "Maybe your plans, but not your life. Charlie, as I remember him, which is vaguely, is a bleeding heart, dying to be loved. He has the face of a handsome baby, doesn't he? Or am I thinking of one of my patients? And Otto is all restraint. So the machine stopped functioning." He shrugged.

"The truth is—" she began, then paused. He waited. "It wasn't a machine," she said quickly. "That's an appalling view of what happens between people."

"What did you start to say?"

"But are you saying what went on between them was only a mechanical arrangement of opposites, Mike?"

"All right, then, it wasn't. The words don't matter anyhow. Otto didn't seem distressed."

"We'd better go down," she said.

But he had left her and was standing near the window, staring at the floor. As he lifted his head, she saw what he had been looking at. She walked over to him. They both looked at the stone on the floor. There were a few shards of broken glass around it. Mike picked it up. It filled the palm of his hand.

"The drapes must have muffled the sound," he said. They both looked down at the street; the broken pane where the stone had entered was at the height of Mike's brow. "It must have been in the last hour," he said. "I was up an hour ago, getting aspirin for someone, and I stopped by here, I've forgotten why, and I know the stone wasn't here then."

Someone walked by on the street below, a St. Bernard puppy shambling along beside him. In all the windows of the opposite houses, lights shone. Car hoods glinted. Mike and Sophie silently watched a man investigating the contents of his glove compartment. A news truck rumbled by.

"Don't mention it to Flo. I'll clean it up. Who could have done it? What am I supposed to do?" Then he shook his head. "Oh, well, it's nothing." He smiled at her and patted her arm. "Sophie, would you like me to send you to a friend of mine? A friend I think highly of? A first-rate man? Member of the Institute?" He hefted the stone, looked back out the window.

"Thanks, Mike, but no."

"But at least go to the hospital," he said, without looking at her at all. She stared at him a moment, then left the room. Otto was waiting for her at the bottom of the stairs, a glass in his hand. He held it out as she neared the bottom.

"Ginger ale," he said.

THREE

"I'm tired of parties," Otto said in the taxi. "I get so bored. Movie talk bores me. I don't care about Fred Astaire, and he doesn't care about me. I care even less about Fellini. Flo is self-important simply because she knows actors."

"Why did you say you hadn't seen *Death Takes a Holiday*? I know you saw it because we saw it together. And you were crazy about Evelyn Venable. You talked about her for weeks . . . those bones, that fluty voice, you said she looked the way Emily Dickinson should have looked . . . don't you remember?"

"My God!"

"And Fredric March, you said, was a perfect expression of an American idea of death, a dissipated toff in a black cape."

"You stored all that away?" he asked wonderingly.

"You fell asleep and everyone knew you were asleep. Mike poked me and told me to take you home."

"They were all trying to out-memory each other. It just proved how old we all are."

"You have to make an effort."

"What were you doing upstairs with Mike?"

"He called some doctors about the cat bite."

"He thinks you ought to see someone?" he asked, alarmed.

She held up her hand. "Look how swollen it is!" she said. She flexed her fingers and groaned. "Perhaps if I soak it, the swelling will go down."

"What did the doctor say?"

"Nobody was in. Don't you know you can't get a doctor any more? Don't you know this country is falling apart?"

"Just because you can't get a doctor on Friday evening does not mean the country is falling apart."

"Oh, yes it does. There was a stone in their bedroom. Someone had thrown a stone through the window. It must have happened just before we arrived. Picked up a stone from somewhere and tossed it through the window!" As she was speaking, she took hold of his arm and now, as she became silent, her grip tightened as though only her hand could continue the burden of her thoughts.

"That's awful," he said. The taxi was idling. Otto saw they were home. He paid the driver. Sophie, suddenly animated by a murky but powerful conviction that she knew what was wrong with everything, ran up the steps. But she had to wait for Otto; she didn't have her keys. He climbed the steps slowly, looking at the change in his hand. Sophie's access of energy, so startling as to verge on pain, died at once. As they walked into the dark hall, the telephone rang.

"Who . . . ?" he began. "At this time of night," she said, as Otto went to the phone. But he didn't touch it. It rang three more times, then Sophie pushed past him and grabbed the receiver. Otto went into the kitchen and opened the refrigerator. "Yes?" he heard her say. "Hello, hello, hello?"

No one answered, but there was a faint throb as though darkness had a voice which thumped along the wire. Then she heard an exhalation of breath.

"It's some degenerate," she said loudly. Otto, a piece of cheese in one hand, gestured to her with the other. "Hang up! For God's sake, hang up!"

"A degenerate," she said into the mouthpiece. "An American cretin." Otto stuffed the cheese in his mouth, then snatched the phone from her hand and replaced it with a bang in its cradle. "I don't know what's the matter with you!" he cried.

"You could ask," she said, and began to cry. "I've been poisoned by that cat." They turned to look at the back door.

"My God! It's back!" she exclaimed.

A gray shape was huddled against the bottom of the door, toward which Otto ran, waving his hands and shouting, "Get out!" The cat slowly raised its head and blinked. Sophie shuddered. "I'll call the A.S.P.C.A. tomorrow," Otto said. The cat got up and stretched. They saw its mouth open as it looked up at them hopefully. "We can't have this," Otto muttered. He looked reproachfully at her.

"If I don't feed it, it'll give up," she said mildly.

"If you allow it to . . ." He turned off the living room lamp.

"Why didn't you answer the phone?" she flung back at him as they went up the stairs. "You're becoming an eccentric, like Tanya."

"Tanya! I thought Tanya lived her whole life on the phone."

"She won't answer it any more unless she's just broken off a love affair."

"Love affair," he snorted, following Sophie down the hall to their bedroom. "Tanya and love!"

"She calls up people, though."

"I hate Tanya."

They stood facing each other beside the bed. "You've never told me that," she said. "I've never heard you say that you hated anyone."

"I only just realized it."

"What about Claire?"

"Claire is all right. What do you care what I think about Tanya? You don't like her yourself. You hardly ever see her."

"I hardly ever see anyone."

"Why do you make me feel it's my fault?"

"You haven't explained about not answering the phone," she said accusingly.

"Because I never hear anything on it that I want to hear any more."

They were both standing rigidly, each half-consciously amassing evidence against the other, charges that would counterbalance the exasperation that neither could fathom. Then he asked her directly why she was angry. She said she wasn't angry at all; it was just so tiresome of him to indulge himself about the telephone, to stand there so stupidly while it rang, to force her to do it.

"Let's go to bed," he said wearily.

She gave him an ironic look, which he ignored. She was really wondering what would happen if she told him the telephone call, that sinister breathing, had frightened her. He would have said, "Don't be foolish!" she concluded. "Stop telling me I'm foolish," she wanted to shout.

He was hanging up his suit. She watched him straighten the

pants. "You ought to throw out the underwear you're wearing," she said. "It's about to fall apart."

"I like it when they get so soft, after I've had them a long time."

He sounded rather plaintive. She felt kinder toward him. There was something funny about people's private little preferences and indulgences, something secretive and childlike and silly. She laughed at him and his soft old underwear. He looked down at himself, then at her, as he stripped off the shorts. His expression was complacent. Let him be complacent, she thought. At least, they'd avoided a pointless quarrel. She wondered if Tanya had ever tried to seduce Otto. Then she remembered Tanya's only visit to Flynders. Otto had been shocked, morally outraged really, when he had accidentally discovered that Tanya had used every drawer in an immense bureau for the few articles she'd brought with her that weekend. "My God! She has a scarf in one drawer, a pair of stockings in another, one girdle in another. What kind of a woman is it who would use all the drawers in a chest just because they're there?" he had cried to Sophie.

"Tanya *is* pretty awful," Sophie said as Otto got into bed next to her. "I bet she's awful to make love to. I bet she can hardly take her eyes off herself long enough to see who she's in bed with."

"Go to sleep," he pleaded. "You're going to wake me up."

She subsided without complaint. She wasn't irritated with him now, and it didn't seem to matter why she had been. She examined her hand and decided to give it a soaking. It certainly hurt.

WHEN SOPHIE AWOKE, it was 3:00 A.M. Her hand, doubled up beneath her, was like an alien object which had somehow attached itself to her body, something that had clamped itself to her. She lay there for a moment, thinking of the cat, how surprised she'd been, seeing it again, when she and Otto had come home. It had looked so ordinary, just another city stray. What had she expected? That it would have been deranged by its attack on her? That it planned to smash and cuff its way into their house and eat them both up? She got up and went into the bathroom. The swelling, which she had managed to reduce earlier by the long soak in hot water, had returned. She filled the basin and immersed her hand. Then, looking at her face in the mirror over the sink—she didn't want to see what she was doing—she began to press the fingers of her other hand against the swollen mass of skin. When she looked down, the water was clouded. She flexed her fingers, then made a fist.

When she got back into bed, she half threw herself against Otto's back. He groaned.

"My hand is worse," she whispered. He sat up at once.

"We'll call Noel first thing in the morning," he said. "If we have to, we'll drive up to Pelham and drag him to his office. You've got to have that looked at."

"If it isn't any better."

"Anyway." Otto fell back against the pillows. "What time is it?" There were times when he felt he had not had a full night's sleep since he had been married. Sophie seemed to take a special pleasure in night conversations.

"Three. Did you notice how young Mike behaved? How he looked? Did you see that Hungarian ribbon around his forehead, or folk art ribbon, or whatever it was?"

"Don't talk about it," he said sharply. "Just don't bring it up. It only makes me angry. Wait till he tries to get a job."

"He'll never get a job. Mike will fund him. And the hair. He was playing with it all the time I was talking to him. Pleating it, braiding it, stroking it, pulling it."

"What did you talk to him about?"

"Stupid things, stupidly."

"They aren't all that bad," Otto said.

"Water babies. They come out of faucets, not out of people."

"They want to be Negroes," Otto said, yawning.

"I wish I knew what they're up to," she said, suddenly remembering she had told Mike's father that she wanted to be a Jew.

"They've chosen to remain children," he said sleepily, "not knowing that nobody has that option."

What was a child? And how would she know? Where was the child she had been? Who could tell her what she had been like? She had one photograph of herself at four, sitting in a wicker rocker, a child's chair, her legs straight out, in white cotton panties, wearing someone's Panama hat that was too big for her. Who had assembled all those things? Panama hat, wicker chair, white cotton panties? Who had taken that picture? It was already turning yellow. What did young Mike, dirty, mysterious, seemingly indifferent, speaking that hieratic lingo that both insulted and exiled her, have to do with her childhood? With any childhood?

"Otto?" But he was asleep. A car went by. A slight breeze came through the open window, carrying with it the sound of a dog's bark. Then she heard knocking, a fist on wood. She went to the window and looked down at the ledge which hid from view the stoop and anyone who might be standing there.

There was a kind of grunt, then several sharp raps, then a whisper. Had her scalp really moved? She looked back at the bed. Then she went to the hall and down the stairs, her hand held stiffly against the soft folds of her nightgown.

Stopping at the front door, hidden by the curtains which covered the glass insets, she listened and looked. On the other side of the door, a large body swayed, a large head veered toward the door, then away.

"Otto . . ." sighed a voice sadly.

Sophie unlocked the door. Charlie Russel was standing there, one lapel turned up.

"Charlie!"

"Ssh!"

He stepped into the entryway and she closed the door. Then they were close to each other like two people about to embrace. She felt his whole face watching her like an enormous eye. "I've got to talk to Otto," he whispered intensely.

"He's asleep."

"I'm in a terrible state. I have to see him."

"Now? You're crazy."

"Because I couldn't see him a second before now. Because it's taken me all this time, from this morning when I last set eyes on him, to get to the point where I am. I don't care what time it is." He reached out and gripped her arms.

"I won't wake him," she said angrily.

"I will."

"You're going to hurt my hand. A cat bit me."

"I feel murdered," Charlie said, letting go of her all at once and leaning against the wall. "Listen. Let's go out and get a cup of coffee. Now that I think about it, I don't want to see that bastard."

"Does Ruth know where you are?"

"Ruth who?"

"That's some joke," she said. "I don't like wife jokes. They drive me up the wall. Don't make wife jokes to *me*."

He stooped and peered into her face. "You sound mad."

"I am mad," she said.

"Will you? Have a cup of coffee?"

"Yes."

"Let's make a getaway," he said, clapping his hands together.

"I've got to get dressed. Don't make any noise. I'll be right down. There's a chair. Don't move."

She dressed silently; even the sleeves of her blouse, drawn up carefully over her arms, made no sound. It was as though she was only thinking about getting dressed.

Otto lay diagonally across the bed, one knee protruding from beneath the blanket. She brushed her hair quickly and pinned it, reached for a purse on the bureau, then left it there, putting her house keys in her pocket. As she picked up her shoes from the closet and tiptoed from the room, she felt, for a vertiginous moment, an unlawful excitement.

FOUR

They went down the street silently, quickly, like conspirators, speaking only when they had turned a corner and were headed for downtown Brooklyn.

"Where are we going?" he asked. "Is there anything open?"

"I don't know. I've never been around here at this hour. Did you come by subway?"

"No. I took a taxi. He dropped me at the wrong corner, but I was too tired to argue. I walked to your house."

"Did you tell Ruth you were coming?"

"No. I had gone out to a movie. A man who was sitting beside me told me I was talking to myself. I told him not to interrupt, then, and he told me I was fucking up his one night out. So I left and got a taxi and went to a Bickford's, which was full of people talking to themselves. Christ! Look at the paper all over the sidewalks."

"Please. Don't talk to me about garbage."

They had come to an intersection. From the west, bearing down on them with an echoing bang and rattle of mechanical parts, came a bus. It went through the red light. The driver was hunched forward, his arms encircling the wheel, his hands hanging down like paper hands. There was only one passenger, an old woman with dazzling white hair. She looked at once majestic and mindless.

"What is she thinking about?" Sophie said.

"Nothing. She's asleep."

The light changed and changed again. Discarded wrappings and newspapers rustled all around them. A block away, a few figures stood torpidly outside the windows of a lunch counter. As they walked toward it, Sophie could see two men inside, moving briskly as they rinsed out thick white cups and scrubbed a grill. The people outside were simply standing there, watching. Across the street, near a subway exit, a short fat dark man wearing a tiny black hat was staring down at a sewer grating. He had the stunned immobility of a displaced person who had come as far as he could without further instructions.

"It's about to close," Charlie said.

Sophie's first exhilaration was gone. She was worried. Her whole left arm ached. Her excitement at the contrast between her formerly placid partner's-wife friendship with Charlie—no questions, no answers—and their present circumstances, the thought of Otto asleep and unaware, which had given impetus to her flight from the house, had dropped away. Now it was like the labored conversation among guests at a late hour after there is nothing more to say, nothing but ashes in the fireplace, dishes in the sink, a chill in the room, a return to ordinary estrangement.

"Perhaps we'd better give it up," she said.

"No! There must be a hotel open somewhere. Come on . . . we'll try the Heights."

"Your lapel is twisted," she said, turning to look up at him, hoping perhaps to turn him back with a humble domestic observation. He didn't appear to have heard her. He looked apprehensive. Grabbing her arm, he muttered, "Come on, now . . ."

Charlie was a large man, big-boned and substantial, yet limber, as though there were a gyroscope at the center of his torso. She had always liked his walk, a sloping easy placement of one foot after the other, a handsome swing of a walk. He had a good smell. But now, as she saw, as she felt (he was walking so close to her), he was shambling. And he smelled stale, like stale liquor and stale sweat.

"After Bickford's, I went to a bar," he said. "And I got into an argument." Sophie stumbled, and he let go of her arm at once, as though by stumbling she'd forfeited her right to his support. They crossed Livingston and walked in the direction of Adams Street. "There was a man standing next to the stool I was sitting on," he continued. "He had a tart on the stool in front of him, and he was rubbing up against her something fierce, telling her about a boat. She was smiling in a ladylike way but stiffening her back to give him a little more. He said he'd just bought a seventeen-foot sloop and he was going to christen it 'nigger.' He was going to paint the boat's name in black Gothic letters and then he was going to sail it up to Oak Bluffs and moor it right there in the harbor, where all those rich coloreds go for the summer. On the other hand, he said he was considering calling the boat 'nigger pederast' and sailing it in Great South Bay close to Fire Island. So I introduced myself to him and the lady—she was drinking rye and ginger ale through a straw—and said I had a better suggestion for his boat's name. He told me to push off. I told him to call it 'American motherfucker.' She thought that was a great little name and laughed so hard she fell on the bar, but he hauled off to kill me. I twisted his arm behind his fat back, and then I was asked to leave by the authorities."

They came to Adams Street. Far ahead, Sophie saw the arch of the bridge over the East River. All around them were official buildings, with the peculiarly threatening character of large carnivorous mammals momentarily asleep.

"There's Family Court," Charlie said, pointing up the street. "Your husband won't set a foot in there. Too low class. Half my clients spend most of their time in those urine-scented chambers, sitting on broken camp chairs, trying to get an extra seven bucks a week from some poor devil of a colored man for their ten children which he has abandoned because their support cuts into his drinking money, without which he would chop up his equally wretched neighbors with a cleaver. *You just wait!*"

"What do you mean!"

"Oh . . . not you. I didn't mean you, Sophie. I don't know what I meant."

But she thought he did. He was dissembling—in his fashion.

"You know, Otto and I were at Columbia together. We were even in the Army together. Most of my life, we've been together. Do you know what he said to me this morning when I left? He said, 'Lots of luck, fella'! And then he vomited out that hideous little chuckle he's perfected over the last ten years. I turned away and he pushed a button and his secretary came in for dictation. There I was, feeling the way I did when I was eight years old, my first day in camp, and I had made peepee in my pants because some little nature sadist wrapped a milk snake around my neck."

He paused and looked down at her. "Did you say a cat bit you?"

"We'd better cross here. Yes. I did say it."

"I didn't know you had a cat. What is it? One of those oriental genetic freaks that cost $700?"

"You sound like a corkscrew," she said.

"What's that thing over there?"

"A new co-operative they're putting up."

"Now, what about this cat?"

"It was a stray I was determined to feed. And it bit me, stood up on its hind legs and fell upon me. My skin crawls to think about it."

"Have you been to a doctor?"

"No."

"You are crazy, Sophie. When did you have a tetanus shot last?"

"Not so long ago. I got a barn splinter in my foot last summer and I had one then."

"That's a minor matter. It's the other thing . . ."

"Don't talk to me about it. The cat wasn't sick."

"Rabies can take up to five years to incubate."

"THE CAT WASN'T SICK!" she shouted. "Here!" and she held her hand up. "It's a bite, just a bite!"

"Otto should catch it and take it to a vet. They can tell," he said in a conciliating way. "Now calm down."

"Pain frightens me more than dying," Sophie said. "I won't even let them give me painkillers because I'm afraid the pain will win out over them. Then there would be nothing—except pain."

He laughed, and she thought him brutal. Then she laughed, too. A policeman left the darkened entrance of a post office and walked slowly toward them. Charlie put his arm around her and they crossed the wide street and turned up a lane. "Why do I feel like a crook?" he muttered.

"What's the point of seeing Otto?" she asked him suddenly. "There's no point, is there?"

"I want him to acknowledge that something important has happened. Do you know that when people change slowly and irrevocably and everything goes dead, the only way to cure them is a bomb through the window? I can't live that way, as though things were just the same."

"You're the one who left," she said. "He doesn't even know you feel this way."

"No, he doesn't. That's his moral failure."

His face *was* like a handsome baby's, she thought, just as Mike Holstein had said. Once, seeing him whole, as it were, for one brief flash, out in the boat last summer on a buoyant, brilliant day, his blue eyes wide as he looked up the mast to the wind indicator, his hair bleached white by the summer sun, with his pouting mouth and heavy nose, she had thought of a Renaissance *putto*.

"Look, there's a place open," she said. "What do you mean, moral failure? He's like most people."

"I'm not concerned with most people."

"I thought that was your concern, most people."

"Don't haggle with me," he said, pushing open the door. He hurried her inside. "God, I'm cold," he said.

Against the imitation brick wallpaper, a few dim lights cast an orange glow. Somewhere in the gloom, a radio played low, occasionally crackling with static. The bartender, one hand on the bar, the other on a shelf across the way, straddled his narrow arena and cocked his head to watch the silent screen of a small television set, which was suspended from the ceiling.

"Isn't that Alice Faye?" asked Sophie.

The bartender turned to look at her. He smiled. "Old Alice," he said.

They went to a booth but no one came to serve them. Charlie said that what he'd really like was a three-minute egg with a bit of butter in it and a cup of strong black coffee. It's a wish for morning, Sophie thought. He went to the bar and fetched them back two bottles of Danish beer.

As he sat down, a man in the next booth cleared his throat violently. Then he said, "Honesty is my God. Frankly, I wouldn't have lied to Hitler."

There was a kind of female moan of assent. Sophie peered over the back of the booth and saw a woman, her head resting on one hand as though it had come loose from her neck.

"How do you know what Otto feels? What is it you want him to do? You and he have been fighting for years, haven't you? Like smiling people in a swimming pool, kicking each other under water."

"Opinions don't matter in the end," he said dispiritedly. "Affection does . . . loyalty. I've always loved Otto. Today he behaved toward me as though I were the boy who comes to the office with the sandwiches and coffee." He rubbed his eyes violently, then blinked at her. "He's shut up in a box," he said, "Squire Bentwood . . . had to bury his wife . . . dead, you know."

"I'm his wife," she said, "and not buried."

"When his oldest friend takes up with black sharecroppers and other undesirables, he refuses to look. And if his oldest friend leaves his precincts, he doesn't give way to unseemly emotions. He doesn't have unseemly emotions."

"You're a coarse man," she said, startled at her own words. She hadn't thought anything; she'd just been listening, and

suddenly she'd said that. "Coarse," she repeated. He had reared
back; his mouth hung open. It was her own protest against
Otto she'd been hearing, but why, on Charlie's lips, did it have
that special kind of untruth that hides itself so despicably in
virtuous opinions and only indicates the self's vanity? And she
wanted him to tell her Otto was cold, shut away; her desire for
that confirmation was like an aroused and insatiable appetite.
Yet, she'd called him coarse.

"You don't know what's going on," he said at last. "You are
out of the world, tangled in personal life. You won't survive this
. . . what's happening now. People like you . . . stubborn and stupid and drearily enslaved by introspection while the foundation
of their privilege is being blasted out from under them." He
looked calm. He had gotten even.

"I thought that's what you were talking about, about personal life?"

"I was. But my meaning is entirely different from yours."

"But I didn't say anything about personal life," she protested.
"You don't know what I think about anything." Oh, but he did,
she thought. She'd gotten to him with that word. He was, she
could see it in his face—he was trying to look severe—thinking about "coarse."

"Well, perhaps you're just innocent," she suggested.

"Innocent!" he exclaimed. She laughed at once and extrav-
agantly. He looked relieved. "That's the truth. I didn't know
about Lancelot and Guinevere till I was twenty-three."

"That's not what I meant," she said. She clasped the cold bottle of beer in her left hand. Pain flared up. He saw her flinch.

"I'm going to take you to the hospital. There's a good one just
across the bridge."

"Not yet," she said firmly.

"Why not, Sophie? It's simple enough."

"I won't," she said. "I won't go running off to a hospital for something as foolish as this."

"It's foolish not to. You're afraid of those shots, aren't you? Why don't you admit it to yourself?"

"When I said innocent before, I didn't mean sexually," she said sharply. "There are other kinds of innocence."

"Ruth wouldn't agree with you," he said. "She talks about nothing except the 'new liberation.' She's taken up Yoga and chopped off her hair. She wants to get hold of some hashish. I told her to wait and she'll be able to buy it at Bloomingdale's notions counter. She had a revelation last summer . . . she told me about it, how she was standing next to a man she didn't know on the beach. And the sun was at the zenith and the heat was beating down, the ocean in a blue heat haze. She looked at his back—his 'naked back,' she says—and wanted to embrace him. She talks about sexual modalities, she talks about the 'wit' of pornography. She's going crazy, poor devil, and she's driving me crazy. But listen. What's strange is that we've stopped making love. All winter, a cold winter."

Sophie felt a thrill of fear. She didn't want to hear about it, thinking of Ruth, her air of sexual plenty, how Ruth had always made her feel shy, vaguely oppressed. "I haven't spoken to her recently," she said, embarrassed.

"Oh, yes. I know that," he said meaningfully.

"I'll call her."

"Don't. She doesn't know what's going on. I don't tell her much. She's like a demented Sherlock Holmes tracking down the ultimate clue. Sex is at the heart of everything, so morbid and so banal. I haven't got anyone to talk to."

"You're talking to me."

"So I am."

The couple from the next booth passed them, the woman weeping softly. He was a fat white man. She was a Negro. Her eyes were half closed, her mouth drawn downward. Suddenly she widened her eyes and looked directly at Sophie. "I came here from Dayton to see can I live or not," she said. "Shut up," said the man conversationally. They went on, out the door.

"You don't mean the marriage is finished, do you?"

"No!" he said angrily. "No . . . she's not had anyone except me, and she's afraid of age. She's simply not herself now. But she'll come back, the goddamn fool."

"The children?"

"Oh, they're all right. Linda knows things are bad between Ruth and me. But she's too preoccupied with adolescence to worry about anything else. She's got a snotty way of saying *yeah* that drives me up the wall. Do you want another beer? What are you thinking about? It's funny to be here, isn't it? You and me? Drinking beer and betraying our loved ones."

"I'm not betraying anyone."

"We've always been friends, haven't we?" he asked, ignoring her denial. "There's always been something between us, hasn't there? Don't look so scared. Oh, God . . . Otto, Ruth, this country with its death rays and frozen peas . . . I'm not so different from Otto. I want the past, too. I hate planes and cars and rocket ships. But I don't dare . . . I don't dare. Don't you see? This war! Bobby is already sixteen. He can be drafted in a few years. Look at the mess!"

"Sometimes I'm glad we don't have a child," she said.

He didn't seem to have heard her. He slid out from beneath the table and went to the bar, returning with two more bottles of beer.

"I had two miscarriages," she said.

"I know you did," he said, sounding cranky.

"I've got a uterus like a pinball machine, apparently."

"Why didn't you ever adopt a child?"

"We put it off and put it off and now—we're such a settled childless couple."

"It doesn't matter," he said. "They *are* hostages to fortune. I love them and they suffocate me. And it's a business, like everything is these days, the having children business, the radical business, the culture business, the collapse of old values business, the militant business . . . every aberration becomes a style, a business. There's even a failure business."

"Then there's the committed, self-sacrificing lawyer business," she said.

"I wanted only to be like Mr. Jarndyce, really. That is the kind of lawyer I wanted to be," Charlie said, rubbing his scalp furiously at a certain spot as though someone were hammering away from the inside. "You know . . . of *Bleak House.* There is that scene when Esther Summerson is weeping in the coach, and old Jarndyce whips out a plum cake and a pie from his cloak and offers her both of them, and when she refuses, my God, he simply flings them both out the window and says 'Floored again!' What style!" He began to laugh, shouted, "And flung them out the window!" and collapsed in the corner of the booth, choking a little and waving at the bartender, who was staring at them worriedly.

"I think I've got rabies," she said.

"Have a plum pie," he replied, snickering

"You're the one who doesn't care about anything," she said.

"Oh, stop that stupid giggling!"

"I care about everything," he said. "In my desperate fashion. It's desperation that keeps me going. Let's go wake up Otto. I want to tell him about Jarndyce." And he began to laugh again. Then he wiped his face with the back of his hand and looked at her intently. "Are you desperate?" he asked.

"I don't know. I suppose I need something to do. I'm too idle. They sent me a novel to translate and I hated it. Then a few days ago, someone called and wanted to talk about a Marseilles longshoreman who's written some poems. I said I'd think about it, but I didn't. Did you know my father was half-French? And half-alcoholic."

"And your mother?"

"All Californian. She lives in San Francisco and consults astrologers from time to time. It's her only aberration."

"No more family than that?"

"That's all. A second cousin or two in Oakland, my mother's relatives, but no one I'd recognize on the street any more. After my father died, I lost interest, anyhow. Now I'm at the brink, the extinguishing point. After me, my father stopped. It's a sad thought. We just stop, our family . . ."

"No one in France either?"

"I don't think so. Maybe. He never spoke of anyone. I don't even know who his parents were, what his father did. My father was like an orphan."

She smiled at Charlie and then grew silent as she was struck with longing, an unprecedented longing to see her mother. My God . . . she was nearly seventy, pickled in sunshine by now, living that California life, she thought. It had been months since she'd written, but it was so hard to write. Confronted with a sheet of writing paper, she could only fill it with banalities.

Writing to her mother made her feel that she, Sophie, had no life at all. But her mother was an old woman. Surely she ought to honor her age, if nothing else.

"You liked your father?" Charlie was asking.

"I loved him. When I was about ten, I realized he was drunk most of the time. My mother constructed her social life around the idea that he had a slight speech impediment which made him shy. When he was falling down drunk in the living room, she just went away to Sausalito for a few days to visit one of her cronies. The real-estate business they had was in his name. But she ran it. He once told me that the only thing he had ever wanted to do was to play the flute, to work for a good conductor, and sit in the orchestra pit with the other musicians."

"Why didn't he, then?"

"Oh, he wasn't sentimental about it. He'd been lazy with his life, he told me. I didn't know, then, what he meant. I suppose I thought he was talking about practicing. My mother isn't lazy. She's a manifestation of some principle of mindless energy. She's got a horrible little yard full of plants she's yanked up out of the ground, and espaliered dwarf fruit trees, and she wrote me that she's now taking up topiary. She probably still smokes too much and last time I spoke to her on the phone, her voice was still hearty, and last time I saw her she was freckled and sunburnt, and I suppose she's still changing the furniture around the way she used to, knocking the hell out of it while my father watched from the door." She smiled. "She was always in control of something," she continued. "Except for one problem she never could manage. She had a good deal of trouble saying hello. I remember, when visitors came, how she'd back into the room, puffing insanely on a cigarette, looking like a cornered rat until the greetings were over. She never talked to me about my father. Never."

"How did he die?"

"He shot himself with an Italian pistol he'd bought in Rome just before he married her."

"Do you ever see her?"

"Not for the last ten years. I suppose I'll have to one of these days. My father had small, beautiful feet and he was very proud of them. After he died, I found about ten pairs of his shoes gathering dust in a corner of a closet. I could see the print of his arch in the leather—it was very high. They were English shoes, and he had them made specially, like Mike Holstein has those Italian shoes made for himself."

"How is Mike? I liked him, what little I saw of him."

"That's where we went tonight," she said. "Yesterday night." She experienced a wave of weakness and she shook her head very slightly. He reached out a hand toward her. "Are you all right?"

"Tired," she said. "It just came over me. What's Ruth going to think if she wakes up and finds you gone?"

"She'll assume I'm with some pale young beautiful girl, where I ought to be at my age."

"Oh, no, she won't. That's not what she'd feel if she really thought that."

"She doesn't really feel anything these days."

The bartender had tuned up the television set.

"Try the brightener," said a man at the bar. "No, try the vertical."

"I like the oldies," the bartender said. "Imagine seeing Alice Faye after all these years."

"You want to go home, don't you?" Charlie leaned toward her. "Just another few minutes, all right?"

"Soon. I'm worried now. If Otto wakes . . ."

"He'll find it bracing," Charlie said. "Do you want to telephone him?"

"He doesn't like to answer the telephone, even in the daytime. And we had a crank call when we got home from the Holsteins." She looked searchingly at him, close to a conviction that it could have been only he who had called; he'd probably tried for hours and at last, when she'd answered, he'd gotten frightened. How odd if, so passionately intent on confronting Otto, he had become speechless just when there had been an answer.

He was still leaning forward, but his neck and shoulders looked strained, as if he were forced to maintain a posture of intimacy long past the death of the original impulse. "Tell me a story," he said. "I don't want to go home yet."

"You wanted to see Otto," she said. Was she telling him or asking him? The booth was a small chilly room. A dank odor rose from the plastic seat cover. Somewhere within that confined space was the faint smell of pickles. She moved abruptly and felt the plastic sticking to her thighs. The bartender was fiddling with the set. Only two other people sat at the bar, elderly men, neither drunk nor sober. Charlie continued to lean toward her; she began to feel breathless, cornered. She visualized herself creeping up the stairs, taking off her clothes, placing her face between Otto's shoulder blades, advancing into sweet domestic sleep as though into warm water.

"It wasn't you, was it, Charlie, who made that call?"

He sighed and sat back. He didn't answer her question. "I wanted to see Otto. I'll have to see him. He can't get away with it. . . . Five minutes and we'll go. All right? Tell me more about yourself."

"Then I'll tell you about my love affair."

"Yes," he said, nodding. "I'd like to hear about that." He smiled generously. "A recent one?" he asked lightly.

"A few years ago," she said, and was instantly appalled by what she had done. He looked stricken. She had made a mistake. She had imagined their impulsive flight from the house, from Otto, had freed them from the restraints of caution and subterfuge, the habits of daytime life with their toneless and depthless familiarity. She had trusted the circumstance and overlooked the participants. He watched her. She wanted to take back what she had said. "I'm inventing for your entertainment," she said. He reached across the table and took her hand. "That's the hurt one!" she cried and he released it at once.

"Oh, why are you so horrified!" she exclaimed.

"I'm not. It's ordinary," he said. "Only something I took for granted, and unimportant, after all."

"I said I invented it," she said.

He laughed. "All right. But I don't believe you now. I saw the look on your face, especially when you said 'my.' You were excited."

"Oh, God!" she said, and put her hand over her eyes. "Well, there's no story. Ordinary, as you said." She dropped her hand and began to pull her coat over her shoulders.

"At the time, Otto and I were thinking of separating."

"Were you?"

"Otherwise it wouldn't have happened."

"I don't know about that," he said matter of factly.

"I want to go now. My hand hurts dreadfully. If you'll take me to a cab."

"I'll take you all the way home," he said.

They didn't speak in the taxi. But, often, he turned to her; she felt his silent observation and she bore silently, as punishment, the violence of her desire to explain, to mitigate, to extenuate.

As she inserted her key into the lock of the door, she heard Charlie calling softly from the idling taxi and, turning, saw him leaning through the window.

"I did make that phone call," he said, "if it makes you feel any better." Then he rolled up the window and the taxi went on down the street.

Sophie stood motionless in the hall. The living room looked smudged, flat. Objects, their outlines beginning to harden in the growing light, had a shadowy, totemic menace. Chairs, tables, and lamps seemed to have only just assumed their accustomed positions. There was an echo in the air, a peculiar pulsation as of interrupted motion. Of course, it was the hour, the light, her fatigue. Only living things do harm. She sat down suddenly on a Shaker bench. Fourteen shots in the belly. Fourteen days. And even then, there was no guarantee; you died from rabies, you choked to death. What pity could she expect? Who would pity her in her childish terror, her evasion, her pretense that nothing much had happened? Life had been soft for so long a time, edgeless and spongy, and now, here in all its surface banality and submerged horror was this idiot event—her own doing— this undignified confrontation with mortality. She thought of Otto, and ran up the stairs. In the bedroom, Otto lay sleeping, blankets and sheets twisted around his middle, his feet thrust beyond the edge of the bed.

FIVE

Sophie soaked her hand. The hot water pained, then comforted. When she dried her hand, her fingers felt freer, as though the poison of the bite had withdrawn to concentrate on the wound itself. She belched softly, and with a habitual uneasiness at the thought of being overheard in such secret, unrestrained manifestations of bodily being, she looked quickly through the open bathroom door, down the hall.

She was bloated; it must have been the beer. Her body was not her own any more, but had taken off in some direction of its own. In this last year she had discovered that its discomforts, once interpreted, always meant the curtailment, or end, of some pleasure. She could not eat and drink the way she once had. Inexorably, she was being invaded by elements that were both gross and risible. She had only recently realized that one was old for a long time.

She pulled her slip off and dropped it in the straw basket she used for her personal laundry. The unvarnished straw tore her stockings, but she wouldn't replace the basket, either out of inertia or as a small defiance against practicality. She stripped off the rest of her clothes. A bottle of Guerlain perfume had turned to alcohol but still she patted some over her beery belly. Then she went down the hall and into the bedroom, where she found her nightgown on the floor where she had left it.

Charlie would be almost home now, heading toward that populous, gloomy 1920 pile of stone in which he lived. All right, then, he had made the phone call. But why had he made it? And then been silent? Or had he lied? Trying to make her feel better, exchanging a sin for a sin. Had that been Charlie breathing into the phone? Only lunatics did such things. It was going to be a bad gray day; the ashy light in the room was already irritating, like a note of music sustained too long. She looked down at Otto.

Even in sleep he looked reasonable, although the immoderately twisted bedclothes suggested that reason—in sleep—had been attained at a cost. She would wake him, tell him he was well rid of Charlie, who was a man perpetually engaged in establishing his superior capacity for human feeling. He didn't want Otto to grieve at the end of their partnership so much as he wanted him to admit that he, Charlie, was the right sort of human to be—loving bleeder that he was! And now it appalled her to think she had given him that information about herself as carelessly as she might have handed a child a toy.

What was even worse, what humiliated her further, was that she had seen her lover, Francis Early, in much the same way as Charlie saw himself.

There was no way of getting under the blanket without waking Otto. She took a heavy coat from the closet and lay down beneath it. Then she began to tell herself about Francis. She often told herself that story, easing herself into sleep, drifting off as she patched together the ghostly memory of someone in whose real existence she hardly believed any more.

SIX

Sometimes Otto's interest in a client extended beyond the reason that had brought them together. Sophie did not know what particular qualities attracted him; he was not inclined to analyze his own feelings or those of others. He was not inclined to wonder why he liked someone or to talk about what kind of people he thought they were. If Sophie suggested—her voice increasingly exasperated—that so and so amused him because he was unpredictable or naïve or an expert in an obscure field of inquiry (the evolution of amusement parks; black magic in New Orleans), Otto would nod and agree, all the while keeping his finger on the paragraph he had been reading in a book or newspaper. The client was invited to one small dinner party, and Otto would have an occasional lunch or drink with him; that was all. A few lingered on, not close friends, but a little more than clients. Such a one was Francis Early, who had been referred to Otto by a publishing company he represented. Francis himself was a publisher of sorts. His purpose in coming to a lawyer remained ambiguous. If it hadn't, Otto, who detested all divorce litigation, would probably have rejected his "case." Francis' efforts to resolve his matrimonial problems were not energetic. Mainly, he seemed to want to talk about them. Mrs. Early, with her three children, remained holed up in Locust Valley, Long Island, and refused to reply to any legal letters. When Francis phoned her to request she cooperate—at least in the formalities needed for a legal separation—she complained she was having difficulties with the coal furnace; he hadn't given her the right instructions for banking it at night, and when did he intend to have oil heat installed, as he had promised to do several years ago? When Otto phoned her, she muttered, "You go to hell, too!" and hung up.

Francis had left her twice before. The first departure was the one that should have stuck, he told Otto, when there was only one child. Ultimately, Otto gave up any pretense that there was anything for him to do for either of them. Since Francis had a small apartment near Otto's office, they had lunch together now and then.

Francis maintained an office, once the second floor of an opulent town house, on East Sixty-first Street, where, beneath a ceiling of carved plaster that looked like soiled meringue, he published books on gardening, wild flowers, rose horticulture and treillage, along with a line of paperbacks on how to start a collection of butterflies or stamps, sea shells or antique cars, these latter, he said, the nearly exclusive source of the money which enabled him to publish the former.

Sophie had met him the evening she and Otto had gone to see the French National Theater's production of *Andromache*.

She had been aware of a special animation in herself attributed with some truth by Otto to the fact that he would have to wear earphones for the English translation while she could sit there in her bilingual authority. But the more generous truth was that she loved Racine, she loved Jean-Louis Barrault and the adamantine glitter of professionalism of French classical theater productions. She knew, too, that the evening would have a salutory effect on her, for a day or two at least, all that compressed intensity thrusting against her dreaminess; her nebulous preoccupations, qualities which, when he was irritated by her, Otto called somnolence.

Walking up three flights of stairs after a gaudy dinner at a French restaurant, they found Francis waiting for them in front of his door. He was smiling.

He gave them cognac, setting out glasses within easy reach, arranging tables and chairs, speaking all the while, affably and humorously, of the other tenants in his building and his bachelor efforts at housekeeping and, just before he sat down himself, placing on Sophie's lap with easy familiarity a small book of silhouettes of New England wild flowers. His voice was light, rather high, shattered almost comically now and then by a smoker's cough, through which he continued to talk until he ran out of breath. His solicitousness was like an endearment; there was a curious touch of precocity about it like that of an overly conscientious child.

Sophie observed the charred edges of the table where he ate. He must deposit his cigarettes there while he cooked a chop for himself at the three-burner stove. An unwashed frying pan balanced on the edge of the drainboard. There were books heaped on tables—he said he would put up shelves when he had the time to bother—and dusty Venetian blinds at the two windows which faced the street, a couch, some cane chairs, a print of an Edvard Munch engraving on one wall. The door to a tiled box of a bathroom was ajar, and Sophie could see shaving articles laid out neatly on the toilet-tank top.

Otto seemed almost frivolous to her that night, as he bantered mildly with Francis. There was a mysterious character to their apparent liking for each other. But a mystery need not be complex, she thought. Perhaps it was some simple thing that made them comfortable without troubling them with intimacy. Otto didn't have close friends. The long association with Charlie Russel had, even by then, begun to be disfigured by a kind of sullenness between them. Otto had begun to think about Charlie, and what he had said to Sophie expressed a growing contempt of which, she thought, he himself had been hardly aware. The very qualities he had once admired in Russel became the focus of his disapproval. What he had once described as Charlie's warmth and generosity, he now spoke of as impulsiveness and vanity. In a way, Sophie supposed, Otto had defined his own nature by contrasting it with his old friend's. They were a good combination, he had always thought. Where he was inclined to be rigid, Charlie was flexible; where he was literal, Charlie was imaginative. "Christ, he's always *spilling* food on his clothes," he had reported to Sophie one evening. "Just the way he did when we were in college. And I used to want to be like him! I hated myself for being so damned neat! I thought it showed spiritual meanness . . . to be so fastidious." So the erosion had begun.

There was a man in California, a doctor, with whom Otto kept up a lively correspondence, although he rarely saw him unless there was a medical convention in New York. Sophie had thought him a cold man on the one occasion she had met him;

flatulent with country-squire theories of aristocracy and political postures to match. Yet Otto spoke of him with respect, even with fondness.

Perhaps Otto liked Francis because he was so unaffectedly friendly. He was touching. Pleasing.

"I don't know a thing about nature," Sophie said, looking through the book he had given her. "I don't know the name of any bug or tree or wild flower."

Francis was at once concerned, thoughtful. "Jean, my wife," he said, "is indifferent to the things themselves, but she does know the names of everything. It's a peculiar mind . . . that kind. It catches her up, though. She only reads to form opinions and then she can't remember what she's read, only the opinions. I would guess you're quite different." Sophie was vaguely flattered, although what he meant by different she didn't know. Still, she was a little uncomfortable; the flattery was not only ambiguous but in poor taste. But she herself had been disingenuous. She knew the names of many plants and insects and flowers. Why had she offered him false ignorance? To flatter him? Or had he, by placing his book in her lap with facile geniality, irritated her? And had her assertion been made not to show ignorance but indifference to his concerns? They had both been crooked.

They drank brandy and listened to Francis talk about his work. He enjoyed, he said, the benefits of anonymity; he was such an unappetizing bite that no big publisher bothered to eat him up, and he was free not only to publish pretty much what he wanted, but because he stayed strictly away from fiction he escaped the awful exigencies of fashion. He did his little bugs and plants; the natural world was a thousand times more bizarre and interesting than human society. With a charming

smile, he described the manner in which a certain larva managed to insinuate itself into the brain of a songbird in order to
complete its metamorphosis.

"Did you like him?" Otto asked later as they pressed through
the crowded lobby into the theater.

"Yes," she replied. "He's nice, very nice."

"I don't know that he's nice. I would say he's heartless, really.
It's odd. You see how . . . courtly he is, almost old-fashioned. He
affects a large tolerance of the world, he remains cool, he keeps
out of it. I think no one can really be like that—either you're
dismayed and baffled or you reduce everything to aesthetics
or politics or sex sociology or whatever. But Francis—and by
heartless, I don't mean he's hard—has an absolutely impenetrable surface, although he appears to have none at all. He doesn't
take me in, yet I like him. He makes me feel cheerful."

It was, for Otto, a very long dissertation. Sophie looked at him
in surprise. He handed her the program he'd just been given
by an usher who was, at the moment, gesturing impatiently at
their seats. They edged past two men wearing embroidered silk
vests and turned down the seats.

"I've never heard you go on so about anyone," she said.

"That's why," he replied. "Because I like him and I don't see
why I should."

"But are they really going to separate or get a divorce?"

"I don't think so. He's always going out there to see her. He
says she's a realist. I think he means it as a complaint. Maybe it's
the way he says it, with that confiding grin of his."

"Maybe he loves her."

"Love? I don't know about that. In fact, that's where his
heartlessness really shows up. He wants to win. No matter what
he says, I think she threw him out. Oh, he's very dependent on

her . . . she's one of those organizing women, I'd guess, sounded tough to me on the telephone, very tough. There's plenty going on between them all right. He sits up there in his shabby old office and she takes care of the world."

"I wonder why she threw him out."

"I only suspect that. I'm pretty sure he's going to get back somehow. He told me he worries about the neighborhood children coming in to visit his children—they might break something she loves or use her special soap."

"Her soap!"

"English soap. Pears, he said. He's full of peculiar details like that."

She held out to him the earphones for simultaneous translation. "Do you want these?"

"Why imply I have a choice?" he grumbled, and took them.

Despite her concentration on the stage, the first act was somewhat marred for Sophie. Someone had dropped their earphones in apparent discouragement and left, and the tiny flat voice of the translator continued to pick shrilly at the air. The ushers didn't find the earphones until halfway through the play. During intermission, Otto, looking sleepy, wandered off to smoke a cigar. Sophie remained in her seat, aware that the program was slipping off her lap, but curiously inert, as though the cessation of the play had left her with nothing to think about, nothing to do. But just as Otto came down the stairs to their row, she sat up straight, clutching at the glossy edge of the program, thinking so intently about Francis Early that she lost the play until its penultimate moment.

A few weeks later, Sophie arranged to meet Otto and Early at the Morgan Library to see an exhibition of plant and flower drawings. At the last minute Otto called home to say he could not make it.

Long after Francis had returned to Locust Valley, his Munch engraving tucked under an arm, carrying a box of books by a wash-line cord, Sophie wondered what would have happened if Otto had not left them alone together. The answer depended on her mood. But she was unable to deceive herself when it came to recognizing the differing impulses which brought them both to Francis' studio couch. For him, she might have been one of a number of others. But for her, he could only have been himself.

She was thirty-five, too old for romance, she told herself as they got into a taxi on Thirty-ninth Street and Madison. He gave his address. They faced forward rather stiffly. She read the cabdriver's license number and memorized his name, Carl Schunk. They didn't speak. Once Francis took her gloved hand in his and a tremor passed over her and her mouth went dry.

She had, then, an anguished foreknowledge that she would be a long time missing him. But a moment later she forgot; the intensity of her feeling for him obliterated everything except itself. She recalled as in another life, his saying that his wife knew "the name of everything." Had his voice been plaintive? She had not listened cannily enough to understand, and it might have helped her now. But what if he *had* been plaintive? What if his tone of voice had revealed an unalterable attachment? What did she care for Jean, for the house in Locust Valley, the three children, for history, for Otto, for her own past, for what was to happen?

They had been looking down at a glass case, he talking somewhat pedantically about photoengraving, when he had looked at her and smiled. Then he saw that her dazed glance was fixed upon him; he flushed. She saw his blood rise, flooding his neck and his face. He took her wrist in his hand and said, "Oh!"

What she felt then had surely been rapture. He had recognized all at once the violence of the emotion which possessed her, and her gratitude for that recognition obscured for a little time that recognition was the only provision he carried. Her wrist had twisted in his hand, her fingers had reached up and caught his shirt-cuff, then touched his skin. When, years later, she tried to recall the exact sound of his voice, remembering with a certain painful joy that it had been she who had evoked that startled flush, that involuntary *"Oh!,"* she drove herself into despair. The voice would not come back; she could not hear it.

Not long after his lecture near the glass case, Sophie lay next to him on his couch, her head half off the edge, drowsily contemplating her clothes piled up on a cane chair. By lifting her head an inch, she could see his face, so pale now, so mysterious.

She had not ceased to think about him since that evening in the theater. What had recently happened between them on the knobby mattress was as inextricably bound up with her first view of him as it was with the tension which had tightened around her throat like a garrotte, breaking at last into the plangent silence of their undressing, then extinguished by the hasty violence of their embrace. Only now, his thin leg rolled off her thighs. She was moved by the air of transience and neglect in his room, by the smell of dust and lemon—perhaps some lotion that he used, or perhaps two lemons themselves on a table. Light seemed everywhere at once. Passionate endearments rose to her lips, but she didn't speak them. It was not shyness that kept her silent. She tried to force from her consciousness the painful apprehension that the room, except for her own presence, was empty. "Francis?" she whispered. He coughed, one arm reached across her breasts toward a small table, where the fingers found a cigarette, a book of matches. Then it was withdrawn, the momentary warmth of his skin increasing her awareness of the chill that was spreading over her flesh. "It's all right," he murmured. It did not seem he was even speaking to her.

He stroked her arm. Gradually there appeared on his lips that familiar, winning, congenial smile.

On the telephone, they sometimes talked about love. Once, she heard an extraordinary excitement in his voice; she thought she had him, and suddenly freed from the presence of a shapeless and terrible weight, the unlovely issue of their love-making, she spoke without shame of her feeling for him. But when they met again, nothing seemed changed.

But she had her secret hoarding; seeing him as he searched for her in a bar where they met and where she, as usual, was early, watching him as he made coffee on his stove, noting with intense pleasure his long thin back, his slightly stooped shoulders, his sharply drawn profile as he turned from time to time to say something to her.

Later, during a time when there was no room in her thoughts for anything but remorseless obsessive recollection, a perverse desire to debase the tenderness she had felt for him led her to insist to herself that it had all been a kind of fatigued middle-aged prurience. And how she had grown to hate that amicability which had once given her such pleasure! It was a shirt of mail, an expression of his unalterable detachment. Behind it lay his life's desolation, his disappointment in himself, his failure with his wife, his real resentment at his hole-in-the-wall company and his self-contempt for his effort to make a virtue out of limitation. Yet he couldn't seem to help himself—even his bitterness was somehow turned to personal profit. It added

to his mystery; it gave his smile an elusive sadness, and it was
an element in that quality he had of always recognizing the
real meaning that lay behind people's words, as though his soul
attended in the wings of a theater, ready to fly out and embrace
them in universal awareness.

She had once bought him a radio. She had given it to him
in its cardboard box and while he undid the staples, she had
smiled happily because he had said he must get himself a radio
one of these days, because she had anticipated him and gotten
him what he wanted. He accepted it gracefully; his voice was
touched with admiration—he admired thoughtfulness—and
with the suggestion, the merest suggestion, that as a rule no one
bothered to give him a gift, no one troubled, not that he minded.
He was just one of those men who were not given things.

A week later when Sophie came to his room, he had another
radio. He had been astonished, he said, when one of his writers,
a warm-hearted lady naturalist, had simply sent it to him. It
had FM, police calls, God knows what. It was leather-covered
and very swank and powerful. "I can get the world," he said.
Sophie extended her hand toward the radio but didn't touch it.
What had he done with hers? Thrown it out the window?

She would like to have smashed the new radio on his dusty
parquet floor. She smiled instead. She didn't know how to vio-
late that mutual smile of theirs. It was miasmic. It stayed on her
face while she undressed. It would not go away, and she bore it
home with her, a disfiguring rictus.

Only a few weeks after their affair had begun, she suffered
powerful interludes of scorn in which she saw herself to be a
fool, *the fool*. Her shifting judgments on herself revealed to
her how her involvement with Francis had shoved her back
violently into herself. In allowing himself to be loved by her,

he had shown her human loneliness. Yet she had never looked better; the whites of her eyes were as clear as a child's, her dark hair was especially lustrous, and although she didn't eat much, she seemed to be bursting out of her clothes, not because of added weight so much as of galvanized energy. Strain, she thought, became her, tightened up her face which was overly plastic, lightened her rather sallow olive skin. She didn't have a moment of repose, thinking, thinking, thinking about him. She grew arrowy. "You look like an arrow," he said. She had raced to meet him, touched his arm, felt—through jacket and shirt sleeves, even, it seemed, through his flesh—his being draw away from her. Her heart gripped, dropped. He kissed her eyebrow. She inserted her hand between his trousers and his skin, feeling the small high buttock. He laughed and told her a story about a glass worm, how it could be sectioned, and the sections would survive. They drank a glass of white wine. Absently, he touched her ear lobe. She stood up. He backed her against a wall, pulled up her skirt. She tried to anticipate him. He pressed against her, suddenly turned away, showed her a new book on ferns. She heard the zing of a coin as it rolled out of his pocket and hit the floor. On the couch, he knelt above her, looked down at her body with sharp unimpassioned curiosity. He couldn't control a fit of coughing; it rattled her insides, traveled up through belly and stomach and chest. She was outraged that he could make her laugh at that moment. But she couldn't stop laughing. They fell off the bed. Her bones weren't such young bones, and they hurt. "I must give up either smoking or fucking," he said. The gray return was before her. It was unthinkable to leave him. Sometimes she took a taxi. She rode home seeing nothing, her mouth slightly swollen, her cheeks rosy.

It was clear when he had had enough, more than he had ever

wanted. He asked her, did she imagine, had she ever imagined herself on a stage? Why did he ask that? Oh, he didn't know but sometimes the way she spoke, held her head, her emphasis . . . "You mean, histrionic?" Well . . . not exactly.

Then, one late afternoon, he told her he had to go back to Locust Valley. He had to find out what had really gone on in that marriage. If he didn't, how would he ever make another relationship?

"Relationship?"

"I can't marry someone else until I know more about what happened between Jean and me," he said.

"Someone else," cried her inner voice.

He no longer referred mildly to his wife. When he spoke of her, his face grew creased, he looked away from Sophie at some object in the room, the bar, the restaurant. He went to see his children more frequently. He phoned Sophie an hour or two before she was ready to leave the house to go to meet him, and said something had come up. He couldn't see her that day. Next week perhaps.

The last time she rose from his couch, she thought for a single astonishing moment that she was covered with blood, and that the blood was the outline of his body on hers.

What would her life have been if they had gone on together? If she had been that "relationship" he spoke of? It didn't matter. That they would have tired of each other, gone trundling down the worn ruts of sexual boredom and habit didn't matter. She had chosen him at a late moment in her life, when choices were almost always hypothetical. It was a choice out of time.

"He's gone back to Locust Valley," Otto said one evening.

"Who?" she asked foolishly and in anguish.

"Francis has gone back. He'll stay this time, I think." And then he said, "Something of a phony."

"I thought you liked him."

"I do. He's a very appealing fellow. But I think he's a phony. He can't help himself."

Had she finally suffocated Francis? Had he straggled back to Locust Valley because stale air was better than none at all? But what did she know about the air in Locust Valley? And was love suffocation? Yet she could not expunge what she now knew. It was commitment, not even choice, just commitment, and against that rock everything broke, resolutions and desires, words and presumptions. No struggle she could envisage could have torn him loose from that commitment. It didn't matter what his wife was like. It wouldn't, she thought, even have mattered if he had loved her, Sophie.

"What are you thinking about?" Otto asked. It was, from him, an unusual question. Sophie flushed. "Marriage," she said. He smiled, a simple, somewhat abstracted smile.

That they should be sitting across from each other in the same way they had sat for so many years and that the habitual intimacy between them could have suffered so wrenching a violation without there being evidence of it, was harrowing to Sophie. If, all these months, she had so ardently lived a life apart from Otto without his sensing something, it meant that their marriage had run down long before she had met Francis; either that, or worse—once she had stepped outside rules, definitions, there were none. Constructions had no true life. Ticking away inside the carapace of ordinary life and its sketchy agreements was anarchy.

She knew where she had been, she thought. Where had Otto

been? What had he been thinking? Didn't he know *anything*? She looked at him a long time across the table. He did not seem aware of her observation. He was eating a dish of applesauce she had made that afternoon. The spoon clanked softly. There was the lemon-flavored smell of apples. Otto rolled up the corner of his rumpled napkin with his left hand. His eyes, when he glanced across at her, gave back no reflection of what he saw. His forehead was faintly furrowed, his shoulders bent.

He was beginning to speak about the war—a client's son had phoned him to find out what his legal rights were if he declared himself a conscientious objector. Otto refused to talk to him when the boy said he'd like to come and rap with him.

"But you know what rap means, don't you?" she asked.

"Only accidentally. What if I had spoken to him in German, making the fatuous assumption it was up to him to understand me?"

"But he needed help! What does it matter how he asked for it?"

"I told him to talk straight to me. He said 'Wow.' That jelly word! Wow, wow, wow . . . what dogs say to the moon. Then he said he dug me, but he was simply doing his own thing in his own words, and I asked him where the fuck it was written any-one was supposed to do their own thing?"

"Oh, Otto!"

"Oh, shut up!" he shouted, and he shoved himself back from the table and left the dining room. Only a moment after, she had to make an effort of memory to visualize his expression as he had sat there. In anger, he had shouted at her and left the room. But the look she had seen on his face had not been one of anger but of bafflement; the look of one who can find no reason for his affliction.

Sophie did not see Francis until six months later, when he phoned her unexpectedly one day at noon. They were to meet for a drink. He was standing at the bar, reading a book, wearing glasses. "Hello," she said. Her hand reached out to touch his arm, then she withdrew it. "Sophie," he said.

They sat at a small round table, their knees entangled until he turned his chair away. They talked about the book he was reading, a record of Sir Leonard Woolley's excavations in the Turkish Hatay near Antioch. It was his new interest, he said, pre-classical history. And how was she? And what was her new interest? She looked well, he said, thinner, and she smiled, yes, yes, she was thinner than ever. She noted he was wearing glasses now. For reading, he said. The silences between them were a kind of sleep; her eyes tended to close unless she heard his voice. He had coarsened a little, she thought, but she only asked him if he had put on weight.

Perhaps he'd never quite lose that fine fair look about his uncluttered face, that limpidity of expression. It was only a vestigial grace, she told herself, that had survived through adaptation, and been tainted by it.

She told him she'd not been too well. She did not say she had suffered an irreversible loss. Instead, she began, somewhat hesitantly, to catalog her ailments, fatigue, anemia—but saw and was quelled by some suggestion of irony as he listened to her. She could not have said in what it consisted, the faint smile, his narrowed eyes, the slight shift of his body. He put her into a taxi. She looked back through the cab window at him. He was not looking after her but was peering into the window of a shop.

SEVEN

O tto was standing by the window. The sky was ashen. Although she could not see his face, Sophie saw that his attention was focused on something in the street. He held his pajamas in one hand. Naked, next to the jutting edge of a chest of drawers, he looked vulnerable, foreshortened and supplicating. When she rose from the warm bed, only the edge of her fatigue blunted, and went over to him, she saw his expression of somber distaste.

"What time is it?" she asked.

"I don't know . . . around seven maybe," he replied, without looking at her.

She followed the direction of his glance. On the opposite sidewalk, a Negro man reeled silently from stoop to curb and back again. With one hand, he gripped the bunched-up fabric of his pants. In the other, he held a green plastic airplane. His naked buttocks above his wildly rocking legs had a kind of gravity. His sidewise progress suddenly propelled him into the post of a black-painted metal railing. He collapsed, his knees coming together in violent genuflection, his hat falling off, his bare bottom landing on the backs of his heels. He flung one hand into the air, the other gripped the rail, the green plane crushed against it. Then he began to vomit.

A black car rattled past. They saw the Negro, his head fallen back, his eyes shut. His hat, only that second, came to rest in the gutter. With a frenzied lurch, he snapped forward again.

"Don't watch . . ." Sophie begged, pulling at Otto's arm.

"Ssh . . ."

"Come away. Come to bed."

"Wait!"

"You shouldn't watch. It's wrong of you . . ."

"He's fallen into it."

From somewhere behind their house, a dog howled, then a series of anguished yelps followed, slipping and sliding through the still thick gray air. Sophie put her hand on Otto's waist. He felt clammy.

"I wish we could live in a place where they don't torment dogs," she said.

"Versailles," he muttered, then peered at her truculently. "Why are you up so early?" he asked. Without waiting for a reply, he went off to the bathroom. She turned her attention back to the street. The Negro was prostrated in front of a metal garbage can that was chained to the railing he was still gripping. Even as she watched, his hand fell away and flopped onto the pavement, the green plane falling a few feet away. She grew suddenly aware of her own discomfort; her mouth was coated, her body was exhausted and her mind debauched by memory.

She had put herself to sleep again, nursing memories of Francis Early, like an old crone with a bit of rag for a baby. Her arms hung heavily at her sides. The room felt stale. She heard the toilet flushing, then running water, then the padding sound of Otto's feet as he came back to the bedroom. She would like to have gone back to sleep, but she remained standing there in front of the window across which she had drawn the curtains, feeling their grittiness. She realized she'd have to have them cleaned. The Negro shifted slightly.

"God! He's getting up," she said.

Otto sighed and fell into bed, covering himself with the blanket.

"How's the bite?"

"Better, I think," she said, turning on a small table lamp and looking down at her hand. The swelling was still prominent but the redness had diminished. "It's sore. My whole arm is sore. But it looks better."

"You ought to get a tetanus shot today. You can get one any-where." He sounded wearied by the whole subject.

"Oh, it'll be all right," she said, bored with it herself.

He stared at her through half-closed lids. "You do drift, Sophie," he said. "There are certain things one should just do without fuss."

"Maybe he's not drunk. Maybe he's ill," she said.

"He's drunk," Otto said. "Come along to bed."

"How do you *know!*"

"Don't shout."

"Can't you leave room for doubt? Maybe he's had an epileptic fit! A heart attack! You're so full of cunning, catching everyone out . . . the American form of wisdom! What if he *is* drunk! Isn't that bad enough!"

Slowly, Otto drew the blanket up over his head. His legs stuck out beneath it. Her jaws clamped into a vise, Sophie ran to the bed and snatched off his covering. He reached out and grabbed her around the thighs and she fell across him. "You talk too much," he said, "and you're beginning to use 'American' as a pejorative. Do you hate your country?"

"I hate you," she replied.

"A lot?"

"No."

Suddenly drained of the nervous excitement which had made her forget momentarily her tiredness and the monochromatic dullness of this early morning, she buried her face in the edge of the bed. Otto, somewhat apathetically, began to stroke her back beneath her nightgown. She was grateful that they had not fought—she didn't have the energy—but a sullen disappointment roiled about just behind her gratitude. Was Otto going to make love to her while the Negro in the street slept in his own vomit?

She summoned her former lover's ghost. He sat in the straight-backed chair, wearing a brown suède jacket. He wasn't looking at her. A brassière hung over the chair back where she had left it, and Francis leaned forward slightly as though to avoid contact with it. She willed him to sit back. He began to fade away. In Locust Valley, he would be asleep, lying up against Jean, who knew the name of everything. . . . A tear straggled down her cheek. She would never be rid of him. Otto's hand was motionless. She listened to his breathing. He was asleep.

By midmorning, when they awoke, the sky was clear, rosy, hopeful.

"What are you going to do today?" he asked her over breakfast.

"Have lunch with Claire."

"I wish you'd see the doctor."

"I'll call Noel this afternoon."

"You will?"

"He won't be in on Saturday."

"Then the answering service will have him call."

"Answering services are there to muffle the screams of the dying," she said.

"I wish I didn't have to go in today," he said. "Charlie's going has just raised havoc in a small way."

She got up abruptly and carried their dishes to the kitchen. When she returned, he was in the living room looking through his briefcase. She saw a book poking out at an angle and idly reached in and pulled it out to see the title. Then she opened it to a scrap of paper marker.

"Are you reading this?" she asked.

He glanced at the book and nodded. It was *The Death of Ivan Ilyich.*

She went with him to the front door.

"He's gone," she said, looking through the glass insets.

"Who?"

"That Negro man. Just gone."

"An angel carried him away," he said. "The cat hasn't come back, has it?"

"I haven't seen it."

He paused, reached for the doorknob, then touched her hair.

"Did you come down here and read last night? I woke up once and you weren't in bed."

She began to laugh, not wanting to, trying to stop.

"Sophie?"

"I wasn't even here in the house," she said. "Charlie came."

"Charlie!"

"Charlie came here in the middle of the night and wanted to talk. He came to see you, he said. He was a little drunk. We went to a bar on Clark Street." She was still laughing. *Fou rire*, she told herself sternly.

He pulled her back into the hall.

"Why didn't you wake me? Why didn't you say a word until just now when I have to leave?"

"That's why I'm laughing. Because I forgot. I simply forgot."

He dropped his briefcase on the floor. "You're infuriating," he said quietly.

"Why did you say to him, 'lots of luck, fella'?" she asked mulishly, and immediately wished she hadn't. She had felt a stab of impatience with him; her own laughter had upset her, but she hadn't meant to mortify him, and she had, with a report to him on his silliness, not an insult she could take back.

"I'm sorry," she cried. "Oh . . . I'm sorry for that."

His voice was almost inaudible. "Don't bother to tell me anything else. . . ."

"He was angry," she said helplessly. "He was trying to get at you through me. He was hurt because he feels you weren't giving the thing its weight, the end of your partnership . . . that you're indifferent. Oh, I don't know. . . ."

He looked blankly at his wristwatch. "I've done so much of the work for years," he said. His tones were measured, but he was staring fixedly at her shoulder, which felt a faint strain as though he were leaning against it. "Charlie is winsome. There's a kind of flattery, you understand, that he's adept at." He paused. She sensed that he was speaking without much thought and she knew he didn't believe much in the efficacy of words which were, after all, only for what could be said. The truth about people had not much to do with what they said about themselves, or what others said about them. She felt a rush of sympathy for him. He was not able to say what he meant.

"I know," she said quickly. "I know exactly what you mean." It touched her profoundly that neither of them knew. He looked very tired. "Must you go in?" she asked.

"The files . . ." he said. "There's so much to be done. He's taking a lot of business with him. I don't even know yet how many clients."

"You care about him."

"Yes. He got me, too."

"But you have clients who'd rather stay with you."

"Do I?" he smiled faintly. She felt an impulse to tell him about the phone call and Charlie's admission. That she had spent hours with Charlie, being Otto's listless defender, was one thing. But that he had called up and breathed into the telephone like one disordered in mind seemed to her a dangerous piece of information. She didn't know why.

"He wants a new life," Otto said, picking up his briefcase. "Even Charlie wants that." He left then, quite suddenly, shutting the door on her good-bye.

She was startled at his words. *"A new life."* It was one of those melancholy asides people of a certain age were given to. But not Otto.

She wondered if Charlie would try to see Otto today and thought not. With no special sense of how she had arrived at such a conclusion, she was now sure that Charlie did not really want to confront Otto; he was like the stage character who shouts "Let me at him" at a safe distance from his opponent. It occurred to her suddenly that she hadn't mentioned Charlie's phone call because of her own disclosure to him. Why in God's name had she told him!

EIGHT

On Saturdays, the street simmered gently. House owners wore their working clothes; old boys and girls in
faded jeans and paint-spattered shirts cultivated the
earth around the frail young trees on the sidewalk, or stood
and gazed up at their houses with preoccupied stares. One carried a pail or a hose or a paint-brush, another, a scraper for the
drops of paint spotting their new windows, another, a ladder
to rest against the wall to climb and repair a weathered window strip. Both sides of the street were lined with cars, many
of which were small and foreign, some bearing a prominent
label indicating the car had been purchased in Germany or
France or England.

Sophie, looking out from behind the living room curtains,
saw a man hosing down a section of his sidewalk near his stoop.
With rigid arms, he held the nozzle of the hose close to the

pavement and his expression was stern. As she watched, he suddenly dropped the hose and retrieved from the earth around *his* maple the green airplane. He stuffed it into his garbage can, already overflowing, and went back to his hosing.

At the back of the house, dogs imprisoned in small yards ran in circles. Telephone cables, electric wires, and clothes lines crossed and recrossed, giving the houses, light poles, and leafless trees the quality of a contour drawing, one continuous line. The Bentwood yard was covered with gravel threaded by a narrow brick path which branched out to an iron bench painted white, a stone cherub carrying a barely discernible cornucopia and to the lip of a small cement pool. Here and there were several yew trees growing in tubs and patches of mountain laurel which the Bentwoods had stolen, cutting by cutting, from Route 9 on the Jersey shore of the Hudson. Bare spots in the even texture of the gravel testified to the hole digging of cats.

Sophie stood for a moment at the back door. A white-and-gray cat straddled a wooden fence and watched a sparrow, motionless on the limb of an ailanthus tree. She didn't know what she was thinking about as she pressed her forehead against the glass, but she felt a quick apprehension as though someone had walked into the room behind her. The house was silent in a special way on Saturday; she went from window to window, wishing herself dressed and out, yet staring passively at the street as though she were waiting for a sign.

Indolently, she ascended the stairs. Languidly, she dressed. But once on the sidewalk, her mood underwent an abrupt turn; as she walked up Court Street to the Borough Hall subway station, she felt exhilarated. She hadn't told Charlie anything, really. Francis had probably been right about her—she did have a taste for melodrama, and Charlie's nocturnal visit had stimulated it. The cat was healthy. She was going to get away with everything!

Dressed in a coat of French tweed, shod by a Florentine, she waited on the subway platform, her real life as masked as those of the people who strolled past her or leaned against the blackened scarred shafts that supported the ceiling.

Then to her dismay, her eyes filled with tears. She found a handkerchief in her bag and sheltered behind a cold-drink dispenser. There, she found two messages; one, written in chalk, said: *Kiss me someone,* and the other, scratched with a key or a knife, said: *Fuck everybody except Linda.*

In the train she opened the book she had taken from her night table. It was an English edition of *Renée Mauperin.* She stared at a drawing of the Goncourt brothers all the way to Fulton Street. As she turned the pages, her eyes fell upon a sentence: "Illnesses do their work secretly, their ravages are often hidden." It would sound, she thought, less medical and more ominous in French, more universal. She closed the book and tried to pull a glove over her left hand; the pain came at once. It had been there all the time, lying in wait inside her hand. The train was crowded now, and there was the stale, warm, soupy smell of crowds. She could have taken a taxi into the city, but it would have been self-indulgence, made more obnoxious by the fact that she could afford one. Sophie was plagued by a vision of herself sliding effortlessly toward a sickly dependence on bodily comfort. Now, she breathed resolutely of the odious air and covered the throbbing hand with the other. The less attention she gave it, the better.

Before going to Claire's, where she was not expected until noon, Sophie stopped by the Bazaar Provençal, a small kitchen-equipment shop on East Fifty-eighth Street. She wanted an omelet pan—it sat, substantial as its own metal, in a hazy domestic dream: a middle-aged couple sitting together over their *omelette aux fines herbes,* two glasses of white wine, one half of a grape cheese, two pears in a milk glass bowl. . . .

"This one is made better," said an elderly woman, whose sacklike chin was covered with a bristle of stiff gray hairs. "Is it the size you wanted?"

"How big is this?" Sophie asked.

"I'd have to measure it. You've got to season the pan first. You know that?"

Sophie bought instead an hourglass egg timer. Useless. The store smelled of excelsior packing, oiled metal, and the faintly brackish odor of Vallauris pottery. She handed the woman money.

"Your hand is bleeding," the woman observed coldly.

"No, it's not."

"Yes. See? You must have banged it on something."

A single drop of blood oozed from the wound.

"Oh. Perhaps I did."

The woman opened a huge black purse and extracted from it a Kleenex, which she thrust at Sophie.

"We don't have much space in here," she said. "All these new shipments arrived yesterday."

"I didn't do it in here. I'm sure I didn't," Sophie said.

"People have to watch where they're going."

The woman pushed some coins into Sophie's hand. The hairs on her chin were like little metal filings; they appeared to vibrate like antennae in search of prey.

"I'm not blaming you for it," Sophie exclaimed suddenly.

"What! What!" the old woman cried, and threw up her hands as though to ward off a hex. Sophie stuck the unwrapped hourglass in her bag and fled.

Claire Fischer lived in a studio apartment not far from Central Park West. The outer texture of the building suggested powerfully an accretion of natural matter rather than man-made material. The whole surface was covered with dollops of some substance that looked like solidified guano. Beneath the black beams of the lobby's low ceiling, a trickle of light seeped through filthy stained-glass windows. The apartments were all duplexes and commanded enormous rents. Sophie walked up the service stairs to the second floor, where she found Claire's door ajar. She went in and felt, as usual, a disquieting perplexity when she looked at the two-story living room, the oak staircase leading to bedrooms on the balcony above, the marble fireplace with its Victorian grate, the massive shabby furniture. Claire called it thirties-stupid. Sophie sensed that in its profound show of indifference to planning, to decoration, there was an element inimical to her own sense of order: for that same reason, she coveted it. On every available surface Claire had piled her assemblages of shells and stones, dried seaweed, leaves, bits of worn glass and dried plants. The total effect was that of an obsessive attempt to re-create the natural world in miniature, but without design. It was an accumulation, not a display.

"Claire?" said Sophie.

"In here!" came an answering shout.

Sophie went to the kitchen beneath the balcony. Here, the apartment narrowed into sordidness. The kitchen was awful; roach caravans trailed across counters and walls, and the appliances might just as well have been in the city dump. Claire was stooping over a pail near the stove.

"What are you doing? What have you got there?"

"Look at this," Claire said, without changing her stance

or looking up. Sophie stood beside her and looked down into the pail. "That's cornmeal on the top," Claire explained. "The clams at the bottom will come up for it, you see, thereby clearing the sand from their craws. Isn't that ingenious? Of me, not the clams. Did you say hello to Leon?"

"I didn't know he was here," Sophie replied.

Claire straightened up and presented Sophie with her grave, heavily lined face. Her eyes were bright blue, the whites faintly bloodshot. A network of thin red veins spread out from the center of her short blunt nose. When she smiled, as she did now, touching Sophie on the shoulder with one finger, Sophie saw the dim pink inside of her mouth, and little patches of gold where her teeth had been capped. Her short-cropped graying hair stood straight up all over her head. She often ran her hand through that thicket as though to assure herself it was still there. Although she was a heavy woman, she did not look plump—sturdy, rather. Habitually she stood with her feet wide apart, frequently looking down at the floor as though she distrusted its stability. She was dressed in a man's shirt, a skirt made from an Indian cotton throw, white socks and *alpargatas;* the rope sole of one was partly unraveled. A scarf was tied in a knot around her middle.

"He's probably lying down upstairs," she said now. "He's dreadfully tired. I think his wife is driving him into the ground."

"I didn't know he was married again," Sophie said.

"He married a graduate student of his last spring, a dull, dull girl who's convinced herself she's a creature of unbridled lust. That's what he tells me, anyhow. Will you have gin or whisky?"

"Gin."

"He tells me a great deal more than I want to hear about

that side of things. Do you want vermouth or tonic or what? He does like to treat me like his charlady instead of his first bride. He's like most of them though—passionate selflessness until he jumps on you like the old monkey he is."

"Tonic. Why don't you tell him to keep it to himself?"

"That would hurt his feelings. He says she fooled him by writing a very good thesis on Henry James . . . some peculiar angle on his relationship to his brother . . . I don't know. He was lavish in his praise—I'll say that for him, he's generous that way—and the next thing he knew she was swearing there was more between them than a silly old thesis about silly old Henry. He's always been a brain lover, swears he wouldn't touch a woman unless she had a stylish brain. Well, she's absolutely dippy. He hates to go home at night, hides out in the university library. She's always waiting for him behind the door, stark naked, liberated from intellectual concerns, his beast, she calls herself. I met them in the lobby of a theater one evening and she sulked for days, Leon tells me. Sulked over me!" She sniffed. "Sometimes I think there's a goat quartered in this kitchen. Come on, let's get out of here."

In the living room, Claire fell into a monstrous chair covered with a kind of brown bearlike fuzz. Her skirt flew up. In contrast to the rest of her, her legs were thin, and blue veins showed through the white skin.

"You look elegant, Sophie. How are you?"

"Fine . . . no, not so fine."

"Look at those shoes! Made by some European slave for a lira, right? What multitudes we all recline upon! I thought my vanity would subside by the time I was fifty, but it's gotten worse. That's why I dress this way. I'd rather look like an aged go-go girl than a middle-class frump. There used to be a tribe in

Africa that flung women who were fifty over a cliff. But I suppose they've become enlightened by now. How's Otto?"

"The office is in a mess. Charlie Russel is leaving the firm.
Otto doesn't say much about it. Charlie is taking it very hard."

"Otto didn't kick him out, did he?"

Sophie hesitated. "No, it wasn't that. They weren't getting
along."

"Well, then, it's a good thing, isn't it?"

"I don't know. It's been a long association. Charlie seems very
bitter. He talks as if Otto had somehow betrayed him."

"I don't believe that. I wouldn't believe anything Charlie said."

"You don't know anything about him."

"That weekend I spent in Flynders with all of you was enough."

"You sound like Otto," Sophie said sharply. "He doesn't think
about people more than two minutes at a time, then by some
supernatural agency presumes to arrive at total insight."

"Total insight!" repeated Claire, laughing. "Sounds like a
depot in North Dakota. Listen, I'm not claiming any such thing.
In fact, I didn't get Charlie at all—it was the way he offered
himself, like a platter of *antipasto*, then stood back and seemed
to watch one consume it. I didn't like him. His attitudes were
impeccable, all that good liberal stuff spread out before one, so
reassuring, so appetizing, so flattering. I don't like impeccable
attitudes."

"No holy fools enter paradise," said a voice from the ceiling.
Sophie looked up and saw Leon Fischer leaning against the balcony, looking down morosely at Claire. He was fat and yellow-
ish skinned and his blazer jacket was too tight.

"Come on down, Leon," Claire said. "Come and see Sophie."

"I can see her from here," Leon said crossly. "Claire, I

knocked over a box on your dresser. What new madness has taken hold of you?"

"What box?"

"Full of horrible little instruments like bugs. They've all rolled away under the bed and the furniture. I started to pick them up but I was overwhelmed by the dust. Don't you ever clean up around here?"

"No, I don't, Leon."

"What are you doing with all these misshapen little horns and flutes and drums?"

"I play with them," Claire said complacently. "Since I can't afford the large ones, I have small ones."

Leon started down the stairs very slowly, gripping the banister with a hand that looked as soft as a glove full of water.

"Who is a holy fool?" Claire asked, watching his downward progress with a look of intense concern, as though he were a child whose first staircase venture this was.

"I was thinking of my son. I don't know whom Blake had in mind."

"Do you want a drink?"

"No. What have you done with the Château Margaux?"

"It's taken care of."

"What have you done with it?" He walked toward the sofa like a convalescent from surgery, sinking down next to Sophie and emitting an enormous quavering sigh.

"Are you working on anything?" Claire asked Sophie.

"Not at the moment. Perhaps I will, later on."

"How pleasant it must be not to be *working* on anything," said Leon. "How pleasant to read, uncompromised by purpose. You must be rich."

"I don't feel seriously about work any more," Sophie said coldly. "It's not a matter of money."

Leon coughed up a creaking laugh. "If you didn't have money, you'd find it a serious matter," he said.

"I've done a Russian movie," Claire said. "Thank God they're still stuck in realism, Zola-crazy. Subtitling their films is like captioning a child's picture book."

"I'm Zola-crazy," said Leon. "I'm crazy about everything up to January first, 1900. What did you do with that wine, Claire?"

"Why don't you try a translation?" Sophie asked Claire.

"It takes too long. I have no patience for anything except cooking. And the pay is insulting."

"That's because you're rich. The rich are always being insulted by money. . . . Why are you wearing your hair in an Afro, Claire? Why the hell don't you pull yourself together?"

"Go back to your idiot wife, old man," Claire said exasperatedly. "Are you hungry, Sophie? I've done a lovely lunch."

"I should be home," Leon announced to no one in particular. "I should be reading a ghastly M.A. thesis. It tortures me. You can't imagine how it tortures me. . . . The woman is a teacher who wants to advance herself and she hates the subject, which she chose herself, and she hates me. It's all a swindle."

"When Leon and I were married, centuries ago," Claire began, "we went to many meetings and sometimes a meeting turned into a party and I sat at Leon's feet and listened to the men talk. Oh . . . how they talked! It was, I guess, civilized babble. It certainly didn't resemble anything I'd ever heard in Concord where I grew up—and yet, what I remember, all I remember, is not what they all talked about, but the wives, especially the older ones, waiting like pensioners for a personal word or two."

"Nonsense!" said Leon impatiently. "You're being grossly sentimental. You always hated intellectuals because they made you feel like a Gentile poop!"

"Intellectuals!" she cried. "Those dilettantes! Those self-aggrandizing fops!"

"Oh, Claire!" he protested. "Oh, don't talk like that!" He looked genuinely hurt.

"Don't yell at me," she said.

"You upset me. Those were serious people—"

"All right, all right, I'm sorry," she said. He shook his head. They looked for a long time at each other, then Leon, speaking very softly, asked, "Did you put the wine in the icebox? You never learn anything. I'm sure you've stuck it in the icebox."

Claire scowled and shifted in her chair just enough to give the impression she was turning her back on Leon. "Are you going to Flynders for the summer?" she asked Sophie.

"I think we will."

"Your husband is a lawyer, isn't he?" Leon said. "You have children? No? You're better off. I have a son by my second wife. I'm sure you remember her, Claire." He giggled faintly. "He's twenty, with the mind of a newborn. I got a letter from him yesterday—he must have found a stamp in the gutter—which I made the error of reading before my first class—nineteenth-century American fiction—and it was supposed to be . . . a poem. About the great oneness of everything—you ought to read Freud's letter to Romain Rolland on that, by the way—about his father, who denies the oneness of everything, about his prayer for his father to be liberated from his bourgeois bonds. It is his belief that history began in 1948, the year of his birth. I have tried to dissuade him of this delusion, but my knowledge is no match for his ignorance. At the very hint of an idea from me, he smiles at me gently as though I were eternally damned. He wears a rubber band around his hair to keep it out of his eyes when he studies the wall in front of him, where his visions arise, and he lives in a horrible slum house in East Orange. If only he wanted to save something, the world, for example. But he is stupid, stupid. The only foundation of his privilege, me, has to lecture forever on William Dean Howells, who bores me sick. Is that justice?"

"You have no memory," said Claire sadly.

"It's all I do have."

"In 1939, you handed out leaflets on Sixth Avenue. There wasn't a question you didn't have an answer for."

"And you and I lived together," Leon said.

"We never talked about love."

"It wasn't necessary."

"We were all of one sex," she said, laughing wildly.

"Yes, yes. . . ." Leon cried excitedly. "No one paid for us! On Fridays I went to the Bronx and lit candles for my mother, reading on the subway, happy, greedy. And I worked for the Podjerskis and, although they paid me next to nothing, sometimes they asked me for advice because I was a college boy! They drank tea all day long, leaving their greasy fingerprints on the glasses, and they knew all their employees by first name; sometimes they played pinochle with the old man—oh, what was his name?—who ran the turret lathe. On Fridays, they closed the shop early so we could all get home before sunset. Once I cut a slice of salami in front of them with a knife I had just used for cheese, and they screamed with horror, would have fired me outright if I hadn't been going to night school."

"I must reheat the *Potage Fontange*," Claire announced. She retied the scarf around her waist, which had come loose as she smoked and listened, her glance resting on Leon, then on Sophie, with remote interest, like someone who does not particularly care for fish but finds herself imprisoned in an aquarium.

"Why must you dress that way!" Leon exclaimed irritably. "Mother Garbage! Do you think character is an excuse for anything? Oh, you should have seen her in the old days, Margaret . . ."

"Sophie."

"Sophie. What a blue-eyed beauty she was! And moved like lightning, fixed leaking toilet tanks and knew how to repair electric plugs and painted like a pro . . ."

"It was Kemtone," Claire called from the kitchen. "We moved into those awful rooms with busted windows and torn linoleum on the floors, ceilings the color of rotten peaches. . . . I painted everything with it. Remember?"

"She couldn't cook then," he said. "We lived on canned macaroni and bacon and whatever I could steal from my mother, like the salami I used to take for my lunch. What has become of us all?"

"Age," said Claire from the kitchen entrance.

"And so many already dead."

Sophie felt that she was sitting in a rain of ashes. She leaned forward, her head down, her eyes half closed, feeling the soft tide mounting to her knees. The ice had melted in her drink. Leon moved heavily on the sofa beside her. Suddenly she felt his ponderous hand on her shoulder. The fingers moved with the restlessness of an elderly person. She turned toward him. He was looking at her entreatingly.

"She says it's age. No one wants to talk about that, do they? No. Humiliations of the bowels. My own body has turned against me. Did you hear how she said that one word? With that female coziness? Trying to neutralize it?" His hand fell away from Sophie's shoulder.

"There's nothing one can do about it," Sophie said, but he didn't hear her for at the same time he had begun to shout. "You never did pay any attention to me!"

"I always paid attention to you, Leon," Claire said, coming back to the living room, drying her hands slowly with a towel. "I just didn't listen. We are not married any more."

"Damn you! Why didn't you marry again!"

"I didn't feel like it," she said, smiling.

"Ah, the truth, at last!" he cried. "Behind all that frantic energy I thought was so admirable is nothing but monstrous sloth. It takes energy to live with someone else."

"We always wrangle like this," Claire said to Sophie. "Just ignore it, if you can. We can get along nicely when we cook together." She smiled and returned to the kitchen.

"It's all that's left," Leon said in a suddenly weak voice. "It's what is left of civilization. You take raw material and you transform it. That *is* civilization. Physical love is all raw meat. That's why everyone's so preoccupied with it now. I have been told by a colleague ten years older than myself—as if it were possible for *anybody* to be ten years older than I am—that salvation comes from staring at the pubic region of strangers, and freedom, from inducing in myself, by the use of a chemical, the kind of ecstatic lunacy in which I spent most of my adolescence, a condition I attribute solely to the strength of my body at that time and the conviction I had then that I would see socialism in the United States during my lifetime. Now that my bones are weak, my brain is stronger. I don't expect . . . anything. But I cannot *bear* the grotesque, lying piety of my own unhinged contemporaries. One man, a literary star"—and here he broke off, laughed once, choked and shook his head—"oh, yes, a star, told me he only regretted the pill had not yet been developed in his own youth. All those girls who might have been his! In this age of generalized cock, is this the whole revelation toward which my life has been directed? I would, in any case, prefer to contemplate the organ of a horse. It is handsomer, larger and more comic than anything my fellow man has to show. It is the age of baby shit, darling. Don't kid yourself. My privacy has been violated—what I've admired and thought about all my life has been debased. Poor bodies . . . poor evil-smiling gross flesh. Perhaps we're going downhill, all of us." He reached out and pressed her shoulder. "Do you understand me?" he asked.

"A little," she said, looking at his exhausted face, pitying him for his harshness which might be only an old habit of words. Do you understand my suffering? is what he had really asked her. She leaned toward him just a little. He patted her shoulder with something akin to tenderness—perhaps it *was* tenderness, grown clumsy from disuse.

"Come and eat my beautiful soup," said Claire. Leon held Sophie's arm, and she adjusted her pace to conform to his hesitant shuffle. The light which came through the dining room windows was so murky it seemed to have texture. On the bare table were soup bowls with covers shaped like artichokes and huge faded linen napkins of pale apricot. Leon, standing at the head of the table, was smiling. It was the kind of unconscious smile, Sophie thought, that touches the face in the same way that light falls upon it.

They ate the soup and Leon asked, in a tone of such gentle inquiry that Claire shot him a suspicious glance, where she had found fresh sorrel? When they had finished, Claire brought in eggs poached in black butter and a bottle of white Bordeaux.

After a bowl of fruit was placed in the middle of the table and the espresso coffee was poured, Leon seemed to be dozing.

"He's in a state of innocence," Claire whispered to Sophie. Leon grinned sleepily. The strain around his eyes had momentarily disappeared and Sophie saw what he may have looked like so many years before when he had handed out leaflets on Sixth Avenue. She reached for a handful of grapes. Claire, looking idly to see what she had taken from the bowl, touched the back of Sophie's hand with a roughened fingernail. "What's that?"

"A cat bit me."

"Someone you know, I hope."

"It was a stray."

"Have you had it looked at?"

Sophie relinquished the stem of grapes and withdrew her hand. "It's nothing," she said.

"A llama bit me once," said Leon in a dreamy voice. "I reluctantly took Benny to the children's zoo when he was small— it was supposed to be the thing to do—and a dirty demented llama reached over the fence and clamped its jaws on my hand. It was like being bitten by dirty laundry."

"Cat bites are always something," Claire said.

"It's much better," said Sophie.

"The grapes are sour," Leon complained.

"Let me see it. When did it happen?" Claire demanded.

Sophie shook her head, saying decisively, "It's of no consequence."

"You *will* duck into supermarkets, won't you, Claire? God! If I had your leisure, I'd take my shopping sack all over the city before I'd settle for sour grapes."

"Oh, Leon, shut up!"

He rose from the table with startling energy, considering he had seemed to be on the edge of physical collapse. He began to stack plates. Sophie pushed back her chair, ready to help. "No," Claire said. "Don't touch them. He always does them. It's part of the agreement."

The two women stood, for a moment, at the window. A truck went by, a car, a man carrying an empty pail; two short women in tall hats held each other's arms tightly and moved defiantly through invisible crowds.

"Are you ever afraid around here?"

"No," Claire said. "I'm not afraid of anything like that."

"Nothing at all?"

"Not at the moment. Not this week, anyhow."

Plates banged in the kitchen. "Let's go sit down," said Claire. They returned to the living room. "It's this way," Claire said. "If someone shoots me in the street, it will be quick, like that! I'd rather that than be waiting in a hospital operating room for someone to walk down the corridor from the laboratory with the dirty news on a piece of glass."

"Your kitchen sponge looks like a spoiled liver," Leon shouted from the kitchen.

"Use your shirt," Claire said. She contemplated Sophie, who stirred uncomfortably, not knowing why she should feel so. She knew Claire was inclined, at times, to strike a some-what oracular stance—something of a fraud, wasn't she? Still, Sophie fidgeted.

"You haven't called for so long," Claire said at last. "I wondered what hit you. And you know me, I never call anybody."

"I don't know. I felt like seeing you."

"Oh, I'm glad to see you. Things are pretty bleak around here, and there's something luxurious about you that reminds me of nice things. But you're so abstracted. I could feel it all the time Leon and I were doing our crazy show. We've known each other a long time now. Are you back with that man again? Can't remember his name. Maybe you never told me. You were so angry when I told you I thought he sounded ignominious."

"Because you thought I was bad to do what I did . . ."

"Bad, bad, bad," Claire said, smiling. "Yes, I did think that. But it was easy for me to say, I never . . ." She hesitated and turned toward the kitchen, where they could both see Leon cleaning up with the single-minded, controlled ferocity of a performing bear. "I never had anything like that," Claire continued. "I suppose the nearest I've come to it is him." She gestured over her shoulder at the kitchen. "And not when we were married. Not then. But now. You must think it's ridiculous . . . but he touches me, you see. I don't feel that I have enough time left for anything but truth . . . about myself. I think I've never really liked sex. I'll tell you something funny. Sometimes he sleeps here with me. We lie together all night long with our arms around each other, and I wake up in the night and I am happy. It is a kind of loving, isn't it, Sophie? We can just be the way we are, with each other. If he didn't come by to see me, I think I'd blow away like milkweed. Sometimes, in the late afternoons, I sit for hours until evening comes. When it is dark—not that it can ever be really dark in the city—I get up and make myself a little supper, a chop, some frozen lima beans. If he's here, of course, I have to be a gourmet. Days like paper chains. All I've got is that old man whom I dumped twenty years ago after he knocked up a Trotskyite lady vamp named Carla." She leaned forward with sudden intensity. "He's scared," she said softly. "He thinks one of his students might try to drug him. He says they harangue him about drugs all the time. Now he's afraid to have coffee in the cafeteria at the university. He even thinks the faculty dining room might be dangerous. He told me just before you arrived that he now knows how scared old ladies are of being raped. He says that's exactly the way he feels. . . ." She looked back at the kitchen. The corners of her mouth turned down. "Although, God knows, he's been on a trip ever since he married that sex-addled bluestocking of his," she said disgustedly. "Oh . . . you see how it is. I started out with you and ended up with myself."

Claire was waiting for her to say something but Sophie was silent, bemused.

"Sophie?"

"No, no. It ended long ago," Sophie said. "I saw him once. He was polite. That's all. I did want to see you and I was grateful when you asked me to come. I'm depressed by my idleness, I guess."

"Neither of us had children," Claire said, a note of wonder in her voice.

Sophie laughed. "Come off it!" she said brusquely, getting back at Claire for something, perhaps for waking up happy in the middle of the night.

"Well . . . how is Otto?"

"You already asked me that," Sophie replied. "He's fine, considering. I think he's better off than some, perhaps because he's not much given to introspection. He's too preoccupied with fighting off a mysterious effluvium he thinks will drown him. He thinks garbage is an insult directed against him personally, and he's still trying to wash the dishes before we've finished eating."

"What bitchiness!" exclaimed Leon, who was standing in the door, wiping a glass. "No wonder men weep."

"I haven't seen any men weeping," said Claire.

But Sophie felt a tremor that seemed to strike her heart. She knew her face had reddened and her breath was short. She had not meant to sound so . . . baleful. And last night, she had wanted Charlie to go on, implying Otto was inhuman, shut away. "I'm sorry," she said. "Leon is right. When I open my mouth, toads fall out. I'm sorry."

Leon looked surprised, then embarrassed. He held up the glass. "Claire, this is the way to dry a glass!" But the hectoring tone was not in his voice. Claire, murmuring something about a chicken, got up from her chair and went to the kitchen, and Sophie, reluctant to be left alone with the echo of her own words, followed Claire.

"I'd better go," she said dubiously, looking at Leon as he mopped up a counter, and then at Claire, who was staring down at a large roasting chicken in a pan. "No need for you to go," Claire said over her shoulder.

"What are you going to do with that bird?" Leon asked.

"Tarragon and cream," she answered.

"Who's coming?"

"Edgar and his new friend, some hairdresser."

"Can I stay?"

"No."

"What lousy company you keep! And I suppose you'll use those clams you've been torturing and *my wine!*"

Claire, a cigarette drooping from her lips, was sprinkling the chicken; a few cigarette ashes floated down to join the tarragon.

"Fairies!" exclaimed Leon, rinsing the sponge.

"Let's have tea at the Plaza next week," Claire said to Sophie. "I'll dress up and we'll sit in the Palm Court and talk about the war and movies."

"Women that hang out with homosexuals are spiders," said Leon, touching the chicken breast with one soft finger.

"Thanks for lunch, Claire. It was nice to see you, Leon," Sophie said.

Leon laughed. "It's never nice to see me," he said. A hank of gray hair fell over one of his pouchy eyes. With a quick touch, Claire pushed it back over his forehead. He grunted and scowled.

At the door, Claire said, "Take care of your cat problem." She handed Sophie her coat. "What a pretty one! Where is it from? Ireland? France? You carry the globe on your back, Sophie. Don't forget to phone me and don't worry about Charlie and Otto. Otto will be better off on his own. Which reminds me . . . wait!" And she left Sophie abruptly and went up the stairs, taking two at a time, her skirt flying above her white legs. When she returned, she was holding a book. "Otto loaned me that a year ago. Don't tell him, but I didn't finish it. He was so pleased when I said I was interested in reading it. And I was, at the time. I did start it." She handed it over. It was *The Common Law*, by Oliver Wendell Holmes, Jr.

Holding it, Sophie felt she had misplaced Otto, and the book was the only tangible evidence of his continuing existence somewhere. She was filled with foreboding and sadness, and her good-bye to Claire was almost inaudible.

The door closed.

NINE

Sophie ran down the stairs and through the lobby, coming to a breathless halt outside the entrance of the building. A hairpin that had worked loose slipped down the back of her dress and fell out on the sidewalk. She looked at her watch. It was four o'clock. She didn't think that the two of them, back up there on the second floor, would be talking about her. Her visit had been only a slight distraction for them, even a vexation, perhaps. She grew aware that someone was watching her, and looked up to see an old man staring at her idly. A gray poodle sat at his feet. How familiar he looked! A character actor? One of those familiar nameless faces she had seen a dozen times—the Duke, my Lord, is in the hands of the French. She smiled at him and he bowed.

In a hotel lobby on Central Park West, she found a phone booth. She dialed Francis' office. There was no one there today, of course. She hadn't indulged her little vice in a long while. Once again, by electronic extension, she moved among the battered file cabinets, the piles of books, beneath the meringue ceiling. She let the phone ring a long time. Then she called Charlie Russel's number. A child answered. She had a sudden wistful memory of the Russel children years ago, small, profane, and brown, during a summer's visit to Flynders. "Is this Stuart?" she asked. "This is Sophie."

"Okay," said the boy. "You want my mother?"

"Yes."

She heard him shout, "Ma!" He breathed into the phone. "Wait a minute."

"Yes," said Ruth.

"This is Sophie."

"Yes."

"How are you, Ruth?"

"Extremely well."

"I called because of all the trouble. I'm sorry about it."

"What trouble? What are you sorry about?"

"Charlie and Otto . . . the end of all that."

"I wouldn't call it trouble."

Sophie tightened her hand around the receiver.

"How are the children?"

"The children are fabulous."

"Stuart sounded so grown up."

"He is grown up. Fantastic. He's going back to that tennis camp this summer. It's incredible how his self-image improved. It's a very serious camp. I mean, the director knows what tennis *is all about*. Three hours on the court, then an hour of constructive criticism."

"And Bobby? Linda?"

"Bobby is going through a little phase of kleptomania. It'll pass, of course."

"Linda?" whispered Sophie.

"Marvelous! She certainly knows who *she* is."

"Ruth? I feel terrible about the breakup."

There was a long silence. "They'll be better off," Ruth said at last. "I've always thought there was something odd about their dependence on each other. They're big boys now, you know, Sophie . . . mustn't let them be babies. It castrates men."

"And you? Are you really extremely well?" asked Sophie.

There was a click; the operator asked for another dime.

"Couldn't we have lunch?" Sophie said.

"I'm on a diet. I don't eat lunch any more," Ruth said. And then she said—or did she?—Sophie wasn't sure what she'd really heard but it sounded like, "Go away, Sophie." In any case, the phone went dead and she didn't have another dime.

When she got home, Sophie went directly to the phone and called their doctor. He would not be in the office until Tuesday at ten thirty. The answering service had no suggestion to make. She could leave her number, of course, and if it was an emergency . . . Sophie got out the Yellow Pages and phoned six doctors within the area. None was available. One woman suggested she call a policeman.

She poured herself a large drink of whisky and drank it down. Then she went to the back door. The gray cat was hunched up on the lip of the stone threshold, its head at an angle, asleep.

When Otto came home, he discovered Sophie off in a corner of the living room, sitting in a formal chair no one ever sat in, stippled with light and shadow. Her silence and the dining room table set for dinner, which he glimpsed through the living room doors, looked like a set piece arranged for some purpose that had subsequently been forgotten. He had the impression she was weeping without sound, and that perhaps the elements of this forlorn scene had been contrived for his benefit, a domestic lesson that was to elicit from him an apology. He spoke brusquely.

"Why are you sitting there like an orphan?"

She held up a book. "There's a little note in your handwriting in the margin. You must have written it a long time ago. The ink has faded and your handwriting looks somewhat different. But I recognized it. It reminded me of how serious you are. It says 'limitation of liability by statue.' Here. Claire returned it." She got up and came to him, switching on lamps as she moved, and put the book in his hand. She was not crying, the dining room table was set for two, not part of a set, only a detail of their routine. He considered what he thought he had seen, an outsider's view of their life form, inaccurately judged perhaps, but for a second he had not been enmeshed in it, had not been oblivious.

"Let's eat in the living room," he said.

"If you like," she said indifferently.

"How was Claire?"

"As always," she replied. "Leon Fischer was there—you remember him? Her husband long ago?"

"I remember him, that yellow-skinned man who doesn't listen."

"Otto? The cat is back . . . at the door."

"The cat!" He ran through the living room into the dining room, toward the back door. "Don't open it," she called out. "Please don't."

At Otto's thundering approach, the cat stretched and eagerly pressed its face against the glass.

"I'll have to open it," he shouted, and cursed the elaborate sequence of steps needed to unlock the door—hook, key, insert, reach, turn again. The cat yawned and observed him, until he drew back his foot to kick it. Then it whirled away, down the steps, and disappeared soundlessly into the dark below.

"Otto, after dinner, we'll go to the hospital."

He turned quickly to her. "We'll go now," he said angrily, apprehensively.

"No. After we've eaten."

"Then it *has* gotten worse?"

"Not worse. But no better. I thought it had this morning." She appeared calm, resigned, yet her voice was thin, splintery, as though she were barely trying to conceal inner breakage. He put his hand on her arm. She drew away from him.

"It's only a bite," she said.

"You're so worried."

They ate from trays in the living room. Otto was afraid of spilling food on the Goum rug and he had to bend over too far to reach his plate. The room felt faintly hostile, as though it resented this misuse of its given function. Otto felt an obscure anger at the ineluctable force of custom. Why the hell couldn't he eat off the floor if he chose to? Yet he knew it was a violation of his own sense of fitness that was making him irritable.

"It was a silly idea," he conceded reluctantly.

"I guess . . ."

"I don't know what I had in mind."

She laughed shortly, two sharp notes like prongs.

"What's funny?"

"Nothing. Did you see Charlie?"

"I saw his tracks. He spilled a carton of coffee on the rug in his office while he was packing up some books." He looked at her intently, as though trying to gauge her receptivity to what he was about to say, then he set down his tray. "I wonder what you really talked about with him." The mild, speculative tone in which he asked the question suggested that he didn't expect an answer.

"He was drunk and foolish and talked about himself. He was complaining, really, about everything. Ruth, his children—"

"How did we arrive at such a place," he said despairingly, and for a startled second Sophie thought he meant the living room, that his impulse to eat here had been an aberration against which he was now protesting. But then he banged his tray down on the coffee table, and went on talking vehemently, his restless glance lighting on her, the floor, the books. His hands were tightly clasped in his lap.

"We agreed," he said. "We agreed it would be best to dissolve the partnership. We were reasonable. Even Charlie was that . . . we had a meeting . . . discussed procedures. The next day, the very next morning, this rancor appeared, these recriminations against me began. It was like retribution, as though he were punishing me. It hadn't been my idea to end the thing. Charlie was the one who was *radical* about it. I knew there were difficulties. You *know* I knew that! There always are. And I know it's a failure of something in me, that I can't feel more about what preoccupies Charlie. But I think about it. I care about justice . . . I care. But Charlie was *at* me. He said he could tell by the way I looked at them, that I had *contempt* for his clients. My God! It was *Charlie* I had contempt for."

"Why?"

"Because he doesn't mean it," he cried passionately. "Because he wants to be caught up by something, to be swallowed so as not to *think* about anything. And the giveaway is what he's trying to do to me!"

"What is it he's doing?" she cried.

"The way he informs clients about the break . . . the way he behaves toward me in front of the office staff. A man called me last week, someone I've represented for years. I'd given some business of his to Charlie, not complicated, but tedious in a routine way. I had too much on my own desk at the time. Charlie took it, willingly I thought. Well, the man told me that Charlie had told him, oh, very circumspectly, that I was putting the work in on the money clients, where the big fees are, and that he suspected I was having personal trouble because I was neglecting so much routine in the office, that I was allowing the secretaries to handle technical matters that, of course, I would never let them near, as he well knows, and that Charlie thought I'd been very abstracted this last year—he even implied it might be something medical—"

"But you should have gone right to Charlie, called him on it!"

"You don't understand. *He* was indirect, and then the client was so nervous that I only realized later when I was thinking it over, something about the conversation puzzled me, what Charlie had been up to. This client wants to stay with me. But Charlie had made him feel uneasy. It's very effective, making people uneasy. They feel something is wrong and want a change even if it goes against their inclination. I think he's been doing this with everyone, but it's been so ambiguous that I didn't know how to catch him out."

"But if he said you were actually sick?"

"He didn't, though. He buries it in general conversation, not the business end, but the social part . . . you know. For example, he told someone he'd been trying to lose weight, then remarked that I had lost a good deal without dieting. In fact, I was gaunt, he said, and he wished he could be. About money, he simply talked about taxes, and said he and I were both concerned about the accountant we'd been using for years. Oh, why was that? Well, Charlie said, the office was taking in a somewhat different kind of client these last two years. Do you see? Vague suggestions, just enough to make people wonder. That poor man who called me last week didn't even know what Charlie had planted in him. It took me half an hour, with the damn calls piling up on the switchboard, to extract it all from him. It was that business about me being gaunt—so arbitrary, but so convincing. He overreached himself there. He's subtle, prides himself on it, then he becomes suddenly stupid, gets carried away by his own cleverness."

"You should have gone and knocked him down," she said angrily. "You let him get away with it!"

"I can't do that," he said.

"Why can't you!"

"I'm too old to pretend that changes anything."

"But aren't you angry? How can you not be angry?"

"I'm not," he said, and sighed. "I'm not angry. But I can't live this way . . . suspecting everyone."

"You mean me."

"I want him out of the office. He's shit on our friendship, our hard work, our history together."

"Did you mean you suspected me?"

"No, no . . . I just wondered what you and he talked about."

She looked at him defiantly. "He said you were cold and looked down at his clients, his 'black sharecroppers' he called them. He said he loved you and you treated him like a delivery boy. I didn't defend you the way I should have. I don't know why I didn't. Maybe because I've known him so long and the whole thing was peculiarly domestic—like one brother complaining about another."

"Was that it?" he asked, his eyes fixed on hers. She turned her head quickly. At that moment, the doorbell rang. It was too late in the day for Jehovah's Witnesses. They both stood up as the bell rang again, a prolonged, demanding ring. How apprehensive they both were, she thought, like people waiting for bad news. "I'll go," he said.

The door opened to an explosion of babble. A man's voice rose and fell in accents of hysteria. Otto backed into view, followed by a young Negro man waving his hands. His head was cocked at so extreme an angle that it was a wonder the leopard pillbox hat he was wearing didn't fall off. A brilliant red shawl, tied through the shoulder loop of his army shirt, trailed on the floor behind him.

Robbery and murder appeared before her in two short scenes, clicked on and off like pictures projected on a screen.

". . . just want to use your phone, man. Like everyone around here thinks black men are *killers!* My God! They been pushing me down their stoops. I got this telegram, I tried to *explain* to the people, and my roommate and I got no phone, that my mother's had a stroke. She lives upstate New York and I've got to get up there. I've got to phone the station, find out when the train leaves. I never seen such inhospitable cats, you know? Man, I'm in trouble and no one wants to help a man in trouble, you know? I just live down a few blocks from here and I can't get to no phone in time! Mrs. Villela closed her bodega early tonight and she always lets me the phone. You know Mrs. Villela? So, please——"

"Yes, yes," Otto said. "Use the phone. Take it easy. It's in here."

Both men disappeared. A minute or so later, Sophie heard the Negro asking for train times and the price of the fare in the same high monotone of panic and demand. After a short silence, she heard whispering. The Negro appeared suddenly in the hall in front of the living room. With an elaborate gesture, he snatched off his hat, smiled violently at her and nodded his head rapidly.

"You got a decent man there, ma'am. A decent man. Oh, I thank you both for this. There's *some* people in the world that's not crazy, and I thank you and your good husband for that." He disappeared like a dancer who had done his turn. Otto glanced hastily in at her and followed the man to the door. "Decent!" she heard him cry again. "A decent man . . ."

Looking flustered, Otto came back to the living room, a piece of brown paper in his hand.

"I gave him $11," he said. "I shouldn't have done that. He said he needed the fare and was temporarily short. He did call Grand Central. I even heard the dispatcher's voice. He said he'd return it to me as soon as he got back and could collect himself. Look. He wrote his address down here."

They both peered at the piece of paper, torn from a grocery sack. "I can't read it," Otto said.

"It says Arthur Weinstein," she said. "But I can't read the street name. Did he say that was *his* name?"

"His roommate's," Otto said. "He didn't want to write down his own, I guess."

"Maybe he thought it wouldn't count," she said.

"I wouldn't say that," he said sardonically. "I would say he's extremely resourceful."

"But his story might be true."

"I don't believe it."

"But it's not so strange a story, Otto. It's ordinary. And what if it wasn't true? What is $11?"

"You mean, *they* are not to be held accountable?"

"I didn't mean that. I meant, when you give someone something, give it."

"He couldn't have done better if he'd held a gun in his hands."

"He could have done a lot better. Oh, what do you care!"

"It embarrassed me, for both our sakes, his and mine. But it was a good invention . . . because it was so ordinary. He even had a place picked out to ask about."

"What makes you think he was lying?"

"My prejudices, I suppose," Otto said.

She went upstairs to get her purse and change her shoes. She wasn't thinking about anything now except the hospital.

TEN

At the hospital information desk, a powdery old clerk told them to go back to the street and walk around to the emergency-room entrance a block away. There was no access from here, she said. She had the spurious helpfulness of an airline stewardess. Her smile did not conceal from Sophie her judgment: emergency cases belonged to a low social order in the hierarchy of disease. They left the reception room quickly, both of them unpleasantly aware of the special claustrophobic warmth that seems to be the natural climate of illness.

The night was smoky and damp; they walked through mist that was like sweat on an invisible surface. At the door of the emergency room, a policeman stood on one leg, his other foot pressed back against the brick wall, his face devoid of expression. They pushed open the rubber-rimmed doors and found themselves in a long corridor at the end of which was a high desk like a cashier's stand in a restaurant. Behind it sat a man who was engaged in looking importantly at some papers on a clipboard. Just to his rear was the entrance to a waiting room. Although he did not look up as they approached, it was clear he knew of their presence. His head began a small reluctant lateral movement until, at last, with a resigned sigh, he faced them directly. He had a pencil mustache and a repellent patchy hairline, bare in one place, thick outcrops of hair in another.

"Yes?" he said. "Name?"

Before either Sophie or Otto could answer, the desk phone rang. The man picked it up and began a long indolent conversation with God knows who—marked by frequent bursts of laughter which caused his upper lip to disappear and brought the black line of his mustache hairs to just over his small teeth. The Bentwoods stood with their chins at the edge of the desk, and when Sophie turned once to glance helplessly at Otto, she wondered if she, too, looked so reduced in size.

He put down the phone at last. "Name!" he demanded crossly, as if they should have answered hours before. Otto gave their name, address, and telephone number in tones of aristocratic chilliness, but when the man asked if they had medical insurance, Otto attacked his pockets brutally as if he were mugging himself. He finally produced the little card with its numbered categories.

"Now," said the man, looking up from the form in which he had been writing down Bentwood particulars. "What's the trouble?"

"A cat bit me," Sophie replied.

"Ah ha!" snapped the man. "And where did this cat bite you?"

"The hand."

"Which hand?" he asked with elaborate patience.

"Left hand."

"When?"

"Friday."

"Friday! You mean it bit you Friday?"

"Yes."

"You shouldna waited this long. Go sit in the waiting room. You'll be called." He picked up his phone again, and Otto and Sophie went limply into the waiting room.

It was like a bus station, an abandoned lot, the aisles in the coaches of the old B. & O. trains, subway platforms, police stations. It combined the transient quality, the disheveled atmosphere of a public terminal with the immediately apprehended terror of a way station to disaster.

It was a dead hole, smelling of synthetic leather and disinfectant, both of which odors seemed to emanate from the torn scratched material of the seats that lined three walls. It smelled of the tobacco ashes which had flooded the two standing metal ashtrays. On the chromium lip of one, a cigar butt gleamed wetly like a chewed piece of beef. There was the smell of peanut shells and of the waxy candy wrappers that littered the floor, the smell of old newspapers, dry, inky, smothering and faintly like a urinal, the smell of sweat from armpits and groins and backs and faces, pouring out and drying up in the lifeless air, the smell of clothes—cleaning fluids imbedded in fabric and blooming horridly in the warm sweetish air, picking at the nostrils like thorns—all the exudations of human flesh, a bouquet of animal being, flowing out, drying up, but leaving a peculiar and ineradicable odor of despair in the room as though chemistry was transformed into spirit, an ascension of a kind.

Against the fourth wall stood a long rickety table on which lay a few torn magazines. The pages of one fluttered in a blast of heat which came from the vent of a metal box which was suspended from the ceiling. Light issuing from spotlights in the ceiling was sour and blinding like sick breath.

There was in that room an underlying confusion in the function of the senses. Smell became color, color became smell. Mute stared at mute so intently they might have been listening with their eyes, and hearing grew preternaturally acute, yet waited only for the familiar syllables of surnames. Taste died, mouths opened in the negative drowsiness of waiting.

Two children lay asleep on the seats. Their father, his head back, his mouth slack, groaned regularly. His wife huddled next to him, her small head tied up in a scarf, her legs, covered with black hairs, not quite touching the floor. She was small and dark and knobby, and looked so uneasy she appeared to be the only person in the room who had taken shelter in it—as though she had come from an even more dismaying place. Next to her, three men sat squeezed together, each wearing a short-brimmed black hat. The middle one had his arm in a crude sling and he kept his glance on the wall clock, watching the second hand fixedly as it swept around and around. Across from the three was an elderly well-dressed woman with a heavily bandaged leg. She played distractedly with the curved handle of a black cane and once she banged it against one of the standing ashtrays. The groaning man snapped his head forward, clutched his belly and glowered at her. The old woman tightened her scalloped mouth and very gently, but deliberately, tapped the ashtray again.

"Let's go," whispered Sophie urgently. "I'll go to Noel on Tuesday. It won't make any difference now. There's no need for us to sit here." Otto grabbed her upper arm and squeezed it violently. "Put up with it!" he demanded through gritted teeth. "Put up with it!" he repeated. "Everyone else does."

An hour later, perhaps two, the children were awakened by their mother when she tried to accompany her husband into the treatment room. Her husband, letting go of his belly for a minute, shoved her back on the bench. The older child giggled and punched her brother in the neck. He began to cry noisily and the woman held her jaw as though she had a toothache. Then she stood up again. The man spoke to her rapidly in Spanish while the nurse who had come to get him watched with murderous patience. Only Sophie looked up at the weeping child, the man, beginning to shout now, the stubborn figure of the small woman. The rest of the wounded averted their eyes from the scene; their attention continued to rest upon the second hand of the clock, the black cane, the magazine pages riffled by the hot air from the vent.

At last the woman sank back on the bench. The boy put his head on her lap, wiping his nose with her skirt. Soon, the man returned, waving a piece of paper, a bullying look of cheerfulness on his face. The woman with the cane was summoned, and eventually limped back through the waiting room on her way out, a new bandage around her leg. The three men remained, silent, expressionless, looking like extras on a set, hired and then forgotten.

"What if someone were bleeding to death?" whispered Sophie. Otto didn't answer. He had fallen asleep, his chin sunk in his collar.

"Mrs. Bentwood!" the nurse said from the door. Otto sprang to his feet. Perhaps he had not been asleep, Sophie thought, but had pretended to be because he couldn't bear her, couldn't bear another word from her. "You needn't go," she said. "Come on!" he said and grabbed her arm.

The treatment room was divided into compartments by

white curtains moved on runners. In the center of the room was a large U-shaped counter which held charts, bottles, retorts, several telephones and a small dented coffeepot. There were several patients in the room, who must have been there a long time. An old woman was soaking her hand in a washbasin of sudsy liquid, staring straight ahead and biting her lower lip. The thin white hairs on each side of her forehead rose and fell as two nurses walked back and forth quickly in front of her. A man with a bloody gash in his leg was staring at it, as was a dark-skinned young doctor, who might have been a West Indian. Leaning against a radiator, his jacket unbuttoned, a toothless hospital guard was talking and grinning teasingly at a nurse as she prepared a hypodermic. The nurse who had brought in the Bentwoods left them and disappeared behind a curtain. Orderlies moved indifferently around them. But after the desolation of the waiting room, this room had a powerful atmosphere of welcome. Here was conversation, work, solutions.

A Negro attendant, a stocky man with a square head, dark-amber skin, and small bright eyes gleaming out of a network of red veins, walked up to Sophie and stared at her thoughtfully.

"All right, honey," he said. "Now. You the one got bit by the cat, right? Now show it to me, honey."

As she held out her hand, the man with the gash in his leg emitted a short rusty scream as though he'd realized only that minute he was justified in crying out. "No, no . . ." said the doctor softly.

"I'm not gonna take that hand away from you," the Negro said coaxingly. She felt that old-time reassurance that she had once thought the natural property of dark people—as though they were superior caretakers of frail white flesh. Her hand arrested midway between them, she looked intently at him, perceiving for a second the existence of a world of unknown opinion about herself, her clothes and skin and odor. Then she thrust her hand at him. "Oh, yeah," he said reflectively. "I see it."

A nurse with a face that looked as if it had been drawn by a child with a pink crayon, peered over the Negro's shoulder at Sophie's hand, then said something to an orderly who was standing next to the counter. He reached for the telephone and dialed a number.

"We've got to report it, you know," said the nurse.

"Report it?" Otto echoed.

The alarm in his voice extended Sophie's own, and she moved uneasily away from him.

"What do you mean?" she asked the nurse sharply.

"To the police. Of course we have to report it. All animal bites have to be." She shook her head sternly, then repeated, "We have to report it."

"What's her name?" asked the orderly impatiently. The nurse picked up a piece of paper. "Mrs. Sophie Bentwood," she replied, spelling out the name and giving the address. Then she returned back to Sophie.

"Now, when did this happen?"

"Yesterday."

"Yesterday? Why didn't you come in then! Yesterday!"

"I didn't think it was necessary."

"Oh, were you wrong!" said the nurse.

"Roll up your sleeve, dear," said the Negro.

"What for?" asked Sophie, childish, paranoid, ashamed.

"A little tetanus, honey. Just roll up your sleeve, dear, and the nurse will take care of it." He waited patiently until she had done what he'd told her to do and then went over to the old woman, whose face softened into hopefulness at his approach.

Another nurse, jolly, sloppy-mouthed, looked at Sophie's hand, resting now on the counter like an exhibit.

"Guess it's not the best time to ask, but you wouldn't like a kitten, would you? A lovely Persian kitten? A friend of mine's cat had three and she's got one left."

The guard laughed. "She don't want no cat right now," he said. At that moment, a bed was wheeled past by an orderly; on it lay a small black man, doubled up, his cheek resting on his hand, his eyes wide open and glassy. Another orderly sprang to the doors and pushed them open and the bed shot through into the corridor.

"Relax!" said a nurse in Sophie's ear. It was a fast shot and she didn't feel it. She breathed deeply, flushed. It was over—she was out of it.

"You'll have to have the shots," said the nurse. She had put the syringe down on the counter and was leaning toward Sophie, who caught an aroma of ironed fabric, deodorant and a gamy private smell that seemed to emanate from the nurse's tightly curled ginger-colored hair.

The nightmare of her expectation shriveled into hard realization. She glanced at Otto; the pity in his face belonged to the moment before she had heard the news. It was of no use to her now.

"You get them at the Board of Health," said the nurse. "All you have to do is go there and they'll take care of it." Everyone was watching her openly. She felt their expectation as a kind of leaning forward—the way a cluster of people will lean over someone who has been in an accident. Then the nurse smiled and touched her lightly on the shoulder. The other people, the guard, the orderlies, went back to whatever they were doing.

"I had them myself," the nurse said. "Take it easy. They aren't so bad."

"Not bad?" said Sophie loudly. "Oh, come on! Not bad? Shots right into your belly?"

"Oh, they don't do it that way now," the nurse said. "You get them in your arm. I'm not kidding you. They really aren't bad."

"Was it a cat?" asked Sophie distractedly. She was sure the nurse had lied about the shots.

"You can roll your sleeve down now. No, it wasn't a cat. I was going home one night and ran into a pack of dogs. One of them bit me. It wasn't a bad bite but it broke the skin. It was pretty dark where it happened so I couldn't see the dogs enough to know which one had done it. Not that I was in the mood to go chase them."

"But the cat isn't sick. I know it isn't sick."

"You can't tell by looking," said the nurse, and her voice had altered. The note of sympathy was gone. She had felt Sophie's recalcitrance as a personal quirk she was not obligated to deal with.

"We'll be able to catch the cat," Otto said.

"Oh, well!" the nurse said. "That's a different story. If you catch it, all you have to do is to take it to the A.S.P.C.A. They'll examine it and give the results to the police. You won't have to do a thing, not even lift a telephone."

The dark-skinned doctor was standing at the counter looking at her. He shook his head very faintly. "You'd better have an antibiotic," he said, and began to write out a prescription.

"They really aren't bad, then?" Sophie asked the nurse appeasingly, thinking to herself, I have no pride, no resources, no religion, nothing—why don't I shut up? Why don't I shut up!

"It's boring," said the nurse. "You have to go there every day for a couple of weeks. But it's worth it. I mean, the disease is so *horrible!* I never saw anybody had it but I read up on it after what happened to me. Naturally, I was interested." She turned away and began to read a chart. The Bentwoods were being dismissed. Across from them, the Negro attendant was bending over the old woman. "Let's see your hand, dear. Let's just see it. I won't take it away from you. Ah, that's a good girl. Oh, better. Much better!"

There was a loud buzz, suddenly strangled, and a yellow light flashed in one of three bulbs attached to the wall.

"Yellow alert!" said the guard, watching the flashing light.

"What's that?" Sophie asked of the attendant who was about to open the door for her.

"Someone's passed away," he said.

"Dead," said Sophie.

"Maybe," he said. "They call it here cardiac arrest. They've got a team, 'arrest stat' they call it. And when they hear that buzzer, they run for the patient, throw him on the floor and pound him, make sure he's dead, then if he's not, they've got their ways of starting things up again." He seemed about to laugh, then glanced over his shoulder at the old woman and darted off to her again. She was sitting motionless, her hand in her lap. He picked it up, soapy and lifeless-looking in his dark hand. Otto went through the door but Sophie paused, looking back.

"Let's not horse around, dear," said the attendant to the old woman, and he plunged her hand into the sudsy water.

"We're going to get the cat," Otto said as they got into the car. "Don't worry any more. I'm glad you got the shot. That's all there's going to be."

"Did you ever know that? That when someone dies, that buzzer goes off like an alarm clock?"

"I never thought about it."

"My father told me that in France, in the villages, the church bell is tolled when someone dies."

"That's kinder," he said, then added somewhat sardonically, "it puts a little romance into death."

"Oh, Otto!" she cried. "I'll have to have those shots!"

"No, you won't."

"The nurse had them. Why shouldn't I? I'm so ashamed to make this fuss, this noise."

"It's all right. Make all the noise you want. If it helps. But you've got to draw a line. This is just a medical procedure. You're not in danger . . . it's only an incident. Not death. You don't draw enough lines."

"Why am I like that?" she asked sadly.

"I don't know . . . perhaps you'd have been better off in a village where the bell tolls."

"How will we catch that animal?"

"It'll come back for food."

"It's a good thing I fed it, after all. Otherwise we wouldn't be able to lure it back with food." She managed a pale smile, lost somewhere in the car's upholstery. He must have sensed the smile. He laughed with relief.

"There's a lot to be said for logic," he said. "Even when it's lunatic."

They found a drugstore open on Atlantic Avenue. Several depressed-looking people stood around waiting while the two pharmacists performed behind a glass partition. The deadly overhead light fell upon the usual assortment of drugstore perquisites.

"Where's your Medicaid I.D.?" asked a middle-aged druggist brusquely of a man who stood dreamily in front of the counter. The man started. He looked bewildered, as though awakened for brutal reasons.

"You know I can't fill this," the druggist said, handing a slip of paper back over the counter. "You've got to give me your I.D. What's the matter? You haven't got it?"

The man didn't move. He appeared unable to summon up the words, an explanation to deal with opposition, but there was in his stance a vague determination to oppose the vagaries of official procedure if only with his continued presence. The druggist made an impatient sound and looked around him to the Bentwoods. "Yes?" Otto handed over the prescription.

The man with the missing I.D. didn't move. Then, just as Sophie's capsules were handed over to her, the man walked resolutely to the door. He dropped his own prescription on the floor. "Shit, shit, shit . . ." he said without emphasis, even, it seemed, without anger.

"They'll have to kill the cat, won't they?" Sophie asked Otto, as they drew up in front of the house.

"I think so," Otto said. "But I don't know much about it. They have to look at its brain."

"I've killed the cat," she said.

"We haven't caught it yet," he said.

ELEVEN

"Tomorrow, I'll take you to Flynders," Otto promised. "It's going to be a nice day. I think it's only a kind of spring mist tonight. We'll leave early and we can have lunch at the inn in Quogue. We'll walk around a bit and think about different things. It'll do you good."

Sophie turned on a lamp. "If it comes back . . ."

"It will."

"I may have frightened it away for good," she said, going to the back door.

"Because it attacked you?"

"Well—it knew *something* happened."

"All in a day's scrounging, for a wild thing like that. It doesn't *know* anything except where food is."

She peered through the door. The yard was in darkness except for a streak of light from a window across the way which glistened on the wet surface of a fence. Otto came in from the kitchen holding a bowl.

"Look. The chicken livers. If they don't bring it back . . . Do we have a box somewhere? A good strong carton?"

"We must. You're aways saving everything."

"Go look upstairs, will you? I'll put the bowl outside."

"Don't do that, Otto. Some other cat will come and steal off with the livers." She looked at him as he stood before her with the bowl held out in his hands like an offering. He was utterly absorbed in an intention she thought preposterous. Perhaps it was the nature of that intention itself that made her see them both as fools. How quickly the husk of adult life, its *importance,* was shattered by the thrust of what was, all at once, real and imperative and absurd.

"Not a chance," he said, "because I'm going to stay here and keep watch." He opened the door and deposited the bowl just below the ledge, then went and got a chair and his briefcase from the living room. Full of his plan, he smiled at her confidently and unwrapped a cigar. Perhaps he was right, right to be the way he was.

"I'm ready," he said. "Get the box, Sophie. Go on, now . . ."

By eleven, the cat had not appeared. Otto brought the bowl of livers inside and set it down next to the cardboard box Sophie had found in the storage closet. He moved purposefully, as though to show her that everything was going along according to plan. "It'll be back in the morning," he said firmly.

"For God's sake—be a little *uncertain!*"

He ignored her. He went to empty his cigar ashes in the kitchen, returned the chair to the living room and checked the front door.

"We should leave at nine. We can be in Flynders by noon."

"I'm going to wait here. I *have* to," she said.

He glanced at her. "Your eyes are red. Better not read tonight."

"I can't, anyhow."

"I'm going to turn off the lights in the kitchen."

While he was gone, the gray cat appeared.

"Otto!"

He ran back to the dining room. "Don't open the door yet. Wait . . . I've got to get the livers in the box. Wait a minute."

"You've got to leave one out so he can smell it."

"Look out! I'm going to open the door."

"Put it on the ledge. . . ."

"I know what to do. Ready?"

"Not yet." She ran to the coat closet and fetched back two pairs of Otto's gloves. Rather self-consciously, she gave him the new sheepskin ones, putting her hands into his old chamois pair. "I've been bitten," she said. The cat watched them quietly, only its tail switching slightly.

"Now!" she said.

He opened the door. The cat mewled delicately. Otto dropped a chicken liver on the porch. It hit the cat's back, then slid off. The animal ate it quickly, frantically, grunting with pleasure, then looked up for more.

"On the ledge, on the ledge . . ." she whispered hastily.

He dropped the bit of meat. The cat hooked it with one claw, tore it from its own paw with another, gulped, and circled agitatedly just at the brink of the door.

"The bowl!"

"*Will you shut up!*" he hissed at her. He held the bowl a foot from the floor. The cat slid over the ledge; its two front feet were on the dining room floor, its head swayed back and forth as it sniffed the air. Sophie shuddered deeply. Otto kept the bowl just out of the animal's reach. The gray length stretched. Otto lowered the bowl slowly into the box, murmuring to the cat, crooning to it. "See, see, here it is, come, here it is. . . ." With a rat's rapid, flat-eyed look, the cat came the rest of the way into the room.

The Bentwoods waited. The cat rubbed its body against the box, clawed it savagely, mewled piteously. Then it began to really work on it—standing up, dropping to its feet, shoving itself against the cardboard surface. Its head turned restlessly and nervously. It seemed unaware of the Bentwoods, who stood motionless a few feet away. Quite suddenly, just as Sophie was wondering how they'd ever get it outside, now that it was loose in the house, the cat leaped into the box.

"Quick!" shouted Otto.

They turned over the flaps. "Hold it, hold it," cried Sophie. "Oh, God! I can't . . . it's pressing up against—"

The box shook violently. Otto, with one free hand, began to wrap washcord around it, letting it fall with a thud after each turn. The cat screamed.

A smell filled their nostrils, acrid, vicious, nauseating.

"Fear," Otto whispered. They stared at each other across the box as they both squatted there in front of the door. Then Otto tied a knot in the heavy line. It was done.

The animal had grown silent. Only the smell of its terror still hung in the air all around them. Sophie breathed shallowly.

"Leave the door open," Otto said.

He carried the box to the front door, then put on his coat. She got hers. "No," he said. "You're not coming. It's not far. For cris-sakes, go to bed, don't think about anything."

She watched through the window as Otto walked to the

car, carrying the box. He put it down on the sidewalk, opened the rear door of the car and shoved in the box. Even from where she was standing, the box looked wet. Perhaps it was only the mist.

But she knew it was not the mist. The cat's body had opened up as though it had been smashed, and it had beshit itself. She looked at her left hand. The swelling had gone down.

On the dining room table, she found the package that contained her medicine. She swallowed down the capsule with Scotch.

When Otto returned an hour later, he found her sitting in an ostrich-sized nest in bed. She had contrived it all with pillows and magazines and books. He began to laugh.

"What are you ready for?"

"Diverting myself," she said. "And it doesn't work."

"The night man at the A.S.P.C.A. said there hadn't been a case of rabies around here in thirty years."

"What do they do to the cat? Do they kill it?"

"I don't know. He took the box away. It was snarling by then, but he didn't seem worried. He just laughed."

"When will I know?"

"Monday."

"Not till then?"

"The doctor, the one who does the examination, doesn't come in until Monday. You don't have to call them, just as the nurse said. If there's anything—there won't be—they will telephone you before noon on Monday. It's really over now."

"But you haven't told me about the cat."

"They don't have to kill them any more," he said, then hesitated. He picked up a magazine that had fallen on the floor and dropped it on the bed. "All they need now to determine whether

the animal is healthy is a sample of its saliva, apparently. But
when he asked me if I wanted the cat back, later, I said no. So
he said that they'll dispose of it."

"Dispose of it?"

"Enough, Sophie."

"All right."

"It was terrible, wasn't it? Getting it in the box?"

"That was terrible."

"I've got to take my coat downstairs."

"Oh, Otto, leave it on the chair."

"I am tired."

"Did it make any noise in the car?"

"None. Nothing until I handed it over to the man."

He looked irresolutely at his coat. "Oh, I'll take it down."

"Nothing will happen if you leave it on the chair just this
once," she said exasperatedly. He dropped it on the chair.

"We were lucky," he said.

"We have all the luck," she said.

Otto always turned off the radiator in the bedroom at the
first faint sign of spring and it was chilly now. He shivered as he
undressed. Then he stood naked, staring at the bed in perplexity. "What is it?" she asked.

"I'm hungry and I don't know what I want."

She made a few suggestions. He continued to look nettled.
Then she said, "Oh, come to bed," and he fell heavily beside her
as though he'd been struck down by a blow. She let the magazines
slide to the floor, then picked up a Balzac novel from her bedside
table. But Madame de Bargeton's ambition and poignant inepti-
tudes did not hold her attention. Her mind slid away from the
page. Otto was asleep beside her. She sat up against her pillows
for a long time, wondering what thing it was she was thinking

about just beneath the feigned attention she was giving to those random *topics* that now drifted through her mind.

Deliberately, she visualized the living room of their Flynders farmhouse, then, blurring that bright familiar place, another room began to form: the skimpy parlor of her childhood, her father and a friend speaking late into the evening while she lay drowsily on the Victorian sofa, listening to the drone of the men's low voices, feeling on her cheek the sting of a horsehair which had worked its way up through the black upholstery, safe and dreaming of the brilliance of her own true grown-up life to come.

She put her hand on her cheek and touched the place where the horsehair had pricked, and she gasped at the force of a memory that could, in the space of a breath taken and released, expunge the distance between sleepy child and exhausted adult, as though, she thought, it had taken all these years to climb the stairs to bed.

TWELVE

At the last moment, they decided to take a picnic lunch. They could build a fire in the living room at Flynders and eat before their own hearth.

The morning did not look promising; the sky was slack and wet looking. Yet there was a kind of festivity in wrapping sandwiches in waxed paper, in rinsing out the Thermos. A few grains of sand spilled from the straw picnic basket onto the kitchen counter.

Sophie had awakened to hope and intensified alarm. The unlikelihood of the cat's being rabid had, mysteriously, increased the horror of the possibility that it might be. She moved quickly, packing the food, making an efficient pile of sheepskin-lined coats and gloves, the car blanket, a copy of *Out of Africa* which she would read to Otto on the way out. It was sure to be colder in Flynders than in the city. In Flynders, there was real weather.

"You feel better," Otto announced with evident relief.

"Yes. It's stopped hurting. But I'm high as a kite, thinking about that phone call—"

"You *can't* be worried about that!"

"There is a possibility."

"It's a formality, not a possibility."

"I found your keys on the couch. You must have dropped them there last night."

"Take your pill."

They drove through miles of Queens, where factories, warehouses, and gas stations squeezed up against two-story, two-family houses so mean and shabby that, by contrast, the ranks of uniform and tidy tombstones rising from cemetery islets that thrust up among the dwellings seemed to offer a more humane future. Sidewalks, brutal slabs of cracked cement, ran for a block or two, then inexplicably petered out, and along the center of the tarmac streets, short lengths of old trolley tracks occasionally gleamed among the potholes. Here and there, the skeleton of a vast new apartment complex sat on the rent ground; tree roots and rocks and earth rolled up around its foundation. Cries of boredom and rage were scrawled across the walls of factories, and among these threats and imprecations, invitations and anatomy lessons, the face of an Alabama presidential candidate stared with sooty dead eyes from his campaign posters, claiming this territory as his own. *His* country, warned the poster— vote for him—pathology calling tenderly to pathology.

There were some churches left, most of them small, of red brick or pocked stucco. But there rose one great baroque Spanish cathedral, its entrance barred by iron gates. It sat in the middle of that crawling, suppurating urban decay like a great chilled eminence, half-dead with its own arrogance.

"I wish there was another way to go to Flynders," Sophie murmured.

"Read to me," urged Otto. "We'll be out of this soon."

"It's so hopelessly ugly."

"Don't look at it," he said quickly.

She opened the book on her lap. "I'm going to need glasses soon," she said, looking down at the page. "Can you still read the telephone directory without trouble?" He was not listening to her. He was staring intently through the windshield at the desolate road ahead.

"Otto?"

"I was thinking of what Charlie would have said if he'd heard me tell you not to look. How he would have pounced on that! What an example of my lack of social conscience!"

"Is your every thought examined in the light of what Charlie would have to say?"

"Do you remember years ago, when people liked to quote Thoreau, that line about the quiet desperation of most men's lives? One morning, a month or so ago, I went to Charlie's office and found him slouched in front of his desk, staring at what he had written in block letters on a piece of paper. It was that quote. I asked him, in what I thought was a light tone—although as you know I'm not so good at that sort of thing—if his life was quietly desperate? I don't know . . . the morning was sunny, sunlight on the rug, and it was cold outside and I wanted everything to be all right. . . . He looked at me with absolute hatred. He said that that quote was a prime example of middle-class self-love. And when I said Thoreau had not intended it as such, he shouted that intention meant *nothing*, all truth resided in what a thing was *used* for. There were clients in the waiting room and the lines were jammed with incoming calls. Charlie looked to me like an Irish gorilla, lurching over his desk, about to murder me. I told him he was full of shit. I was stunned by his loathing of me. Then he brayed that no oppression had ever been so difficult to resist as middle-class oppression, because it wears a thousand faces, even the face of revolution, and that it is an insatiable gut that can even nourish itself on the poison its enemies leave lying about to destroy it. I asked him what alternative he had in mind and he buzzed his secretary and told her to send in his appointment."

"But life *is* desperate," said Sophie almost inaudibly.

"Did you say life is desperate?" Otto asked, leaning toward her. Then suddenly he began to laugh. "Read to me," he said again. "Go on." So as the Mercedes joined the thickening traffic that was making its way east on the highway, Sophie read to Otto about the green hills of Africa.

At midmorning, they stopped for coffee, and sat peacefully and silently in the overheated coffee shop until Otto, attempting to open a plastic container of cream, spilled it all over himself. He began to curse, making an addition to his expletives with the remark that all change was for the worst.

He looked more familiar to Sophie than he had for two days, and she realized suddenly that he had been restraining himself since Friday, restraining his *character* for her sake, as though he had shoved into a closet some disreputable relative whose presence might shatter her. She wanted to reassure him—she was thinking of what to say—when he asked her exactly what Charlie had said to her Friday night.

He would continue to ask her, she thought, and she would continue to be unable to tell him. She no longer remembered what Charlie had said to her Friday night.

"Nothing much about you, except what I've already told you."

"What he said about me doesn't matter. He was up to something just because it was *you* he was talking to."

It was clearing outside. Through the window, she saw a ray of sunshine widen on the roof of their car and on a filthy red Cadillac parked next to it. She looked around the coffee shop aimlessly for the owner. There was a couple sitting at the counter, middle-aged, plump, overdressed.

"What could he be up to with me?"

"Disorder. The creation of disorder."

"You know what you sound like? A person who has just gotten a divorce and is telling himself that his whole married life had been nothing but torment."

Otto sighed. "I suppose so."

They got up, and Otto went to pay the sleepy cashier, who was bathed in sunshine. Sophie passed the middle-aged couple and heard the man say in a fierce mumble, "I.Q. Fuck you! If he doesn't work, who cares how bright he is!" The woman's black chamberpot hat seemed to rise slightly above her head. Her mouth snapped shut as though she'd bitten off a thread.

As they passed it on the way to the Mercedes, Sophie glanced into the window of the Cadillac and saw, side by side on the front seat, a large box of Kleenex and a sleeping Pekingese.

"I want Charlie to be gone," Otto said as he backed away from the coffee shop. "Silent and vanished."

"People always seem to have to make a lot of noise when they leave," she said—except for people like me, she thought privately, remembering how submissively and silently she had slunk away from Francis. But then, there was nothing she could have done about it. Yet, for a bitter moment, she was caught up in the old tormenting question: What if Francis had been available? If the door had swung open, would she have gone through it? She glanced over at Otto. Francis had not only deprived her of himself. He had cheated her of her certainty about Otto.

"Why does he have to destroy me?"

"Is that what he's doing?"

He grunted. "No. But I'm getting bruised . . . people I've known for years asking my secretary about my health. It disgusts me."

"The clients who stay with you will forget about it soon enough. People don't think about other people that much."

"If you're a lawyer, they do. If they're in trouble, they do. I'd be better off if I were more like my father. He based his life on the assumption that nothing would come of anything. And hope broke in upon him the way disappointment breaks in on other people's lives. He hated hope. It unmanned him. Assume the worst, my son, and you'll never be disappointed. . . . I was in the hospital room when he died. He couldn't speak or move, and one side of his face was paralyzed. But he broke through that coma just long enough to give me lopsided smile. I knew what he meant. 'See? See how it all ends?'"

"We take the next exit."

"I know. . . ."

They drove around a cloverleaf and then onto another parkway.

"We're not far now," Otto said cheerfully. "We'll be all right. It may be tight for a bit, with money. Two people I'd counted on have gone with Charlie. There was an exchange of sorts, though." He laughed, and continued, "You should see what I got in trade. I could have told her she'd better go to someone else because I didn't deal with such problems. But she was so damned forlorn. Charlie had neglected her, got bored, I suppose—Charlie gets bored easily—and I decided I'd take her on, just to prove I could, I guess."

"Who?"

"Mrs. Cynthia Kornfeld. She arrived at the office with a fractured index finger and eighteen stitches in her scalp." He accelerated. For Otto, it was a dramatic opening to a story. It occurred to Sophie that he had been excited at the idea of doing something that went against his usual inclination. He glanced over at her, smiling, gauging the effect of his words, perhaps. She laughed back and told him to go on.

"Her husband is a rat—I shouldn't say that, it's the wrong approach—named Abe Kornfeld. Two years ago, he struck it rich. What he had done was to buy up a dozen used typewriters from one of those stores on Canal Street. Then he took them apart and reassembled them in some mangled way and arranged the keyboards so that they spelled out mystic nonsense words. A gallery gave him a show. He got $2,000 for a standard and $1,000 for a portable. That was his first show. He developed categories which allowed him to charge considerably more—a standard Royal, for example, was a lot more than a standard Smith-Corona, but a portable with Japanese characters was worth more than both of them. They'd been living in a floor-through flat on Hudson Street for fifteen years. He turned one room into a factory, and she gave up her substitute teaching— she'd been supporting him while he was a painter—and they began to turn out these things at an extraordinary rate, said it was easy, she'd show me if I wanted to do it myself, and still they couldn't keep up with orders. She was stunned by the money that poured in—and scared. She said she felt it was just another novelty and would drop out of sight as soon as something else came along. But he said it was a breakthrough, that the destruction of a typewriter and its reconstitution, its humanization, as a kind of oracle, was a direct blow at American Philistinism. He broke up his old easel and threw it out on the street, and he tore up all his former work. He began to buy things. A Piaget watch, for example. He removed both hands from it and told her he wouldn't be corrupted by his good fortune if he indulged his taste for luxurious objects but always deformed them enough to ruin their function. The evening he beat her up, he began by arriving home late, just after she'd put the child to bed. She was doing most of the work on the typewriters by then, and she didn't know where he went during the days. He was carrying a copy of *Mein Kampf* that night. When she complained that she was tired and they'd have to get some Chinese food or a pizza for supper, he threw the book at her, then said she couldn't deny that Hitler had had a lot of style. Then he told her that they were having a dinner party. He had already ordered Senegalese food from some joint in the Village, and had invited all the people to whom he had ever owed money. Should she make coffee and a dessert? she asked. He didn't care what she made as long as it wasn't square. She felt something special was required, but she had nothing in the house except several boxes of strawberry Jell-O. She cooked them up and poured them into the biggest bowl she had. Then, instead of bits of fruit, she dropped in nickels and dimes. Whether she was celebrating their new affluence, or making an ironic comment, I don't know. I suspect the former since she is not a woman capable of much irony. When she brought in the dessert, she was applauded by the guests, but Abe flung himself at her and had to be restrained by two painters before he did her serious harm. I guess he must have been sore at her horning in with a joke of her own."

"Is that all? Is that what she wants to divorce him for?"

"She says he will beat her again. And he's been getting ugly with the child, too. Everything has changed in a way that makes it impossible for it to change back. She speaks very slowly and flatly and with absolute conviction."

"And what does he say?"

"Nothing. He's disappeared."

"No one knows where? The gallery? Friends?"

"No one."

"Does that frighten her? He sounds crazy. Maybe he had an accident."

"She is one of those people with remarkable patience, but a terminal point beyond which they never go. She told me she never complained about what he was doing, and never questioned him. Now, she behaves as if she wouldn't care if he did turn up dead."

"Is she pretty?"

He didn't answer right away. Then he said, "I don't really know. I'll look, next time."

"Don't you look at women?" she asked slyly.

He didn't answer her and she didn't repeat her question. She felt a mild estrangement between them, just a little moment of tension. She thought about it, turning it over in her mind as she might have turned over an object in her hands, trying to understand her own intention, which she knew had been disruptive. Why interrupt the pleasant boredom of the drive? The sky was all clear now, a bland, washed blue, and the occasional house that could be glimpsed from the road looked freshly painted and prosperous and eternal; and Sophie thought of the great gray sea of sludge through which they had driven only an hour or so earlier.

"What are you thinking about?" she asked him.

"Oh, my father again. When he was in the room, we all watched what we said. You wouldn't have liked him. He didn't care what people talked about as long as they spoke to the point. And a subject had to be completed before a new one was begun. Thoughts had to be ordered, like boxcars on a track. You could not, when describing a summer in Paris, begin to speak about Istanbul."

"What if you did?"

"He had very prominent knuckles and they would turn white. A change in subject, until *he* thought it had terminated, offended some inner sense of progression. It enraged him. In a similar way, if you were a chemist you could not speak about atonality. You might say you liked it. But no judgments."

"You're right. I wouldn't have liked that."

"Here's our turnoff."

The village of Flynders, from which they were now only two miles, had a winter population of fewer than one hundred families, most of whom were entirely dependent on the summer people for their income. In the full summer swing of July and August, the population swelled to at least two thousand, and last summer this number had been augmented by a group of New York advertising agency people who had purchased an old estate, torn down the thirty-two-room house and outbuildings, subdivided the acreage, and started to build a group of houses that was supposed, eventually, to resemble a French farming community. As Otto drove past the area, a small sign nailed to an elm trunk announced its name—BUDDING GROVE. Sophie saw a sway-backed gray horse standing among the half-built structures.

"There's the architect," she said.

Flynders was on neither the ocean nor the bay so the rents for the old farmhouses that were still available were less than those farther out on the island in the Hamptons. There was no bank; one antique shop managed by an elderly and morose homosexual, who spent his winters in Sicily; an I.G.A. market; three gas stations; a post office in a large shed that also housed a laundromat; a general store (hardware, stationery, tennis shoes in large sizes); two public telephone booths, and a narrow dark restaurant which was open the year around. Old-time summer people made a ritual stop each year to make sure the restaurant's permanent exhibit had not been removed from its window—a plastic piece of apple pie, on top of which decayed from year to year a yellow scoop of Styrofoam.

Once, Flynders had been a town, a center for the neighboring farms. Most of the farmland, abandoned and neglected, had reverted to marsh and had once been a halting place for a myriad of birds. Every summer house had, still, in cupboard or basket or bookcase, worn copies of Roger Tory Peterson's *Field Guide to the Birds*. Then the village people had called in the mosquito-control people. Now there were few birds, and poison ivy and Virginia creeper flourished in the acid earth. The elm blight had destroyed those trees not already harmed by frequent droughts. But in the center of the village, three copper beeches survived, black in the noonday sun, purple in the twilight. Even the villagers prized them, not so rapturously as the summer people, perhaps. One manor house remained unoccupied and unsold. It sat on a small rise, a menacing, ugly house, a barrow, deposited and deserted by some 1920's millionaire and left there to testify to the power of money to create a permanent and quarrelsome unloveliness.

A few young people lived in Flynders, commuting many miles to work in distant towns. They lived in houses which they had bought, off the highway, green or blue or pink boxes stacked up into rooms over two-car garages, with Venetian blinds at the windows. A real-estate agent in Riverhead handled the Flynders rentals and sales.

The Bentwoods' house, a small Victorian farmhouse sitting neatly in the middle of a meadow, was a mile north of the village. Otto had placed around it a low picket fence, not because they had close neighbors, but because he had been compelled by his sense of order to distinguish between what belonged immediately to the house and what belonged to the open fields. From their porch, they could see the barn Otto had bought, which was two meadows away to the east. The little fence had made Sophie restless and she had begun, two summers before, to plant flowers outside it. She was a good gardener, but not a passionate one. She had not the long patience required for ordering a landscape. When something did not survive the summer, she lost interest in it and would not try again.

Otto turned onto their dirt road. The mailbox was lopsided on its wooden post. Ahead of them was the house, its shutters closed, a wicker stool they had forgotten to store, upside down on the porch. The ground was hummocky, denuded-looking, gray. In the summer, the grass was cut by a local man who sold the hay to a stable in Southampton. In one of the leafless maples near the house, a hive-shaped nest from last summer hung like a tumbleweed. They walked up the brick path, Sophie seeing from the corner of her eye a pair of green cotton gloves half-buried in the hard soil near where bee balm grew.

"I forgot the lunch," Otto said, and handed her the key to

the back door. She looked first into the kitchen window. Sunlight lay on the floor, touching the maple runners of the rocking chair. She felt a wave of pure happiness.

The cold inside, the chill of a house empty for many months, had a strange softness to it, faintly suggestive of anesthetic. Sophie walked slowly toward the counter, noting with pleasure an assortment of kitchen toys, most of which were duplicates of those she had in Brooklyn. She picked up a round tin box and shook it to hear the rattle of the cooky cutters inside, then recalled suddenly the face of a summer friend of theirs, a painter who had visited them frequently in August. She recalled how he had picked up each gadget on this counter and held it close to his face, tracing its shape with his fingers and how, when he arrived, he washed his hands in the kitchen sink, using the yellow kitchen soap. She had liked him very much, liked his substantial, handsome face, the way the skin of his hands had gleamed beneath the water from the tap, the way he'd *nudge* things with the unself-conscious and sober curiosity of a child or an especially alert animal. He had, she remembered thinking, a certain kind of self-love, the kind that comes from poverty, perhaps, having nothing else to love. He was very poor, except for ex-wives, of which he had several, and he had many theories of how to manage a life which he described with the calm zealotry of one who has received truths from the sun. He didn't smoke or drink—a little peyote now and then—and as he sat down to one of Sophie's dinners, he would groan in mock horror at the dissipation he was about to indulge in. He hardly ever cooked food any more, he said, and had nearly succeeded in giving up meat and fish. So she had said to him self-consciously that she wished she could give up smoking, but guessed her inability was a "failure of character," and she had been shocked by his mockery when he parroted her voice, making it high and fatuous: "Failure of character, failure of character," he had chirped and laughed at her. When she'd quit cigarettes in the fall, she'd dropped him a note—he'd gone off to spend the winter in some Vermont barn—telling him that her character was improving, but he had never answered her. She was thinking of him now, she realized suddenly, because she was staring at what remained of the object he had liked most, a bottle shaped like a bunch of grapes that had held wine vinegar and which was now lying in fragments on the counter and all around it, stains in the wood where the vinegar had soaked in. She frowned, turned rapidly away from the counter. The pantry door was open, and lying spilled on the floor was a large box of coarse salt, canned goods, a broom plucked of its straws.

She dropped purse and book in the rocking chair and ran through the living room to the front door, which she unlocked and flung open just as Otto took the first step to the porch.

"Someone's been in the house."

He set the straw basket down. "*Here?*" And as astonishment gave way to helpless anger, he repeated "Here" without emphasis or surprise, as though he'd learned all he needed to know in half a minute.

Whoever it was had gotten through the first floor bedroom. The window had been smashed, the shutter torn from its hinges. From the foam-rubber mattress which had been dragged to the floor, the handle of a French chopping knife still protruded. The caning of the dining room chairs had been slashed, sea shells ground to dust on the floor, lamps broken, the Paisley fabric of the couch cover torn into strips, cushions gutted, and over every painting or photograph a giant X had been drawn with barn paint. Upstairs in the bathroom lay a decomposed catbird in the tub, and talcum powder, aspirin, disinfectant, and mouthwash had been emptied on the floor. Clothes had been dragged out of closets and cut crazily with scissors. Books had been torn in half. In the dining room, Sophie found an empty bottle of bourbon beneath the table.

Soon they stopped exclaiming; they picked up things, examined them and dropped them wordlessly. Otto held up the stomped spine of a book for Sophie to observe; Sophie showed him a shard of the Bennington-ware pitcher. He began to right the furniture, to sweep up the broken glass with cardboard backing from a picture. Sophie stacked the canned soups in the pantry and brought the broom handle and head into the living room. Might as well burn it. They met in front of the fireplace where, among the heaped up paperback mysteries and magazines, a hummock of dried feces sat like a rotting toad.

"There must have been more than one," Sophie said.

"A battalion," Otto said. "Let's get out of here."

"We can't leave it—"

"No, no . . . we'll go get Mr. Haynes. That bastard. He must have known about this."

They didn't bother to lock the doors.

Haynes lived a few miles away. He was the Flynders caretaker. He had once had a small potato farm, but it had failed in 1953, and since, by then, Flynders had begun to wake from its thirty-year sleep, during which time it had declined insensibly from town to village and become a summer colony, Haynes made himself useful to the city people. He opened their houses on Memorial Day and closed them in September, and sometimes turned on heat and water for their winter vacations. He also worked as a kind of unofficial contractor, hiring people to do the various odd jobs that turned up.

The Haynes property looked as if it had been assembled by a centrifuge. The house, a gnomish conglomerate pieced together with a variety of materials, actually left the ground at its northeast corner and although, if one stooped, one could see timbers and planks wedged in under the floor, the illusion of imminent collapse was powerful.

Three vehicles in varying stages of deterioration stood on three wheels, on two, on none, in a line more or less directed toward a shed shelter, as though they'd been struck down just before they reached their goal. Only the Ford truck looked as if it might still run. Rubber tires leaned against every surface. Cans, tools, pails, lengths of hose, rusted grills, and summer furniture were spread out in front of the house, presenting a scene of monkeylike distraction—as though each object had been snatched up and then dropped, a second's forgetfulness erasing all memory of original intention. A clothesline was strung across the porch and from it hung a few limp rags. A bicycle with twisted handlebars lay against the steps. And from a small chimney black smoke poured as if, inside the house, the inhabitants were hurriedly burning up still more repellent trash before it drowned them.

As the Bentwoods got out of the car, a huge, seemingly jointless dog bounded toward them from behind the house, dropped to the ground at their feet and rolled over, waving its floppy legs. When Otto stepped aside, muttering, "My God!" the dog moaned joyfully and sprang to its feet. The door on the porch opened, and Mr. Haynes poked out a narrow unshaven face.

"Get outa there, Mamba!" he shouted at the dog. "Why, hello there, Mr. Bentwood, and Mrs. . . . What are you folks doing out here in the backwoods this time of year? Don't tell me summer has climbed up and sneaked in and I didn't even know about it!"

"Hello, Mr. Haynes," said Otto frigidly.

As they stepped uneasily on the rickety boards of the porch, Mr. Haynes slid his head out a little farther and frowned. "Don't let that dog get in," he said. "She's in her season. Too big to let in the house. Go take a seat, Mamba. She don't mind the damp with that coat on her."

He opened the door to let them into the house. "Another present from you summer people," he said, smiling wolfishly. "Found her on the beach over at the bay, dragging around a dead sea gull. You people and your animals! Gawd! If I kept all the ones got left out here, I'd have a zoo."

Neither Sophie nor Otto had ever set foot in the Hayneses' house before. The first thing they saw, on the wall near the door, was a huge ring hung with keys and tacked up next to it, a long list of names and telephone numbers on a piece of yellow paper.

In this dark damp parlor, where they were standing, there was an extraordinary number of small bookcases piled up, as in a warehouse. Whatever Mr. Haynes' income was, he evidently augmented it with the leavings of the summer people.

"Nice little parlor," he said, "but let's go out to the kitchen. That's where we spend our time in the cold weather. It's friendly and warm in there and country folks do love their kitchens."

Sitting around the kitchen table like collapsed sacks of grain were Mrs. Haynes and the three Haynes children, two boys in their late teens, and a girl a few years younger. The girl was immensely fat. From beneath a tangle of burnt-looking fair-ish hair, she was staring down at a copy of *Life* magazine, her mouth open.

"Now, here's Duane and Warren," cried Mr. Haynes gaily. "Believe you met them once before when we fixed up your porch. And that's Connie, the glamour girl, over there. And

of course you know Mrs. Haynes here. These are the Bentwoods, Toddy, in case you don't remember. They've got the old
Klinger place."

"Take a seat," said Mrs. Haynes sternly. "Don't stand there
like that. We're glad to have you."

Since there were no extra chairs, Sophie and Otto continued to
stand in the doorway, until, a moment later, the combined smell
of dog and roast meat and hair and skin, cigarette and wood
smoke, so overwhelmed them, they stepped backward into the
parlor. Mr. Haynes, perhaps attributing their retreat to refine-
ment on their part, cried, "Don't be shy, folks! We're here for
all the world to see!" and, taking each of the Bentwoods by an
arm, shoved them forcibly back into the kitchen. No one, during
Mr. Haynes' declaration, had stirred. Then, at some signal from
his father, Duane rose and stretched, squeezed past Otto and
Sophie and returned shortly with two straight-backed chairs.
He waited with insulting patience for them to move aside so he
could smack the chairs down on the kitchen floor.

The Bentwoods' preoccupation with the violence done to
them temporarily abated as they confronted the scene of frowzy
intimacy before them. The heat from a huge black stove, across
the front of which was written *Iron Duke*, could have warmed
up the whole outdoors. Remains of the Sunday meal were
spread out on the oilcloth-covered table. Both boys were smoking, and they continued to smoke all the time Sophie and Otto
were there, as though in a vicious contest to see who would get
the last Pall Mall from the pack that lay on the table next to a
dish of pickles.

Connie announced, "I'm gonna watch the TV."

"You wait till we finish talking with the Bentwoods," said
Mr. Haynes, scowling at her, then smiling broadly at Otto, as

though his daughter's sullenly stated intention was an example of her charm. But Connie ignored her father. She reached across her mother to the television set which sat amid a welter of laundry on top of a new-looking washing machine. Mrs. Haynes smacked her outstretched hand.

"They don't do a thing you say," Mrs. Haynes said complacently. "All alike, this new generation."

"Now, Toddy, we was just the same," said Mr. Haynes, leering at Sophie. "And we know what they want because we was young once ourselves. Right?"

"Someone got in our house and smashed up everything," Otto said loudly.

Duane and Warren straightened up and regarded the Bentwoods with real interest, as though at last they saw some purpose in their existence. Even Connie stopped pouting and fixed her slightly protuberant eyes on their faces. Mr. Haynes' mouth twitched and his nose reddened.

"Oh, my!" said Mrs. Haynes.

"Well, imagine!" cried her husband. "I can hardly believe it. We haven't had anything like that happen around here. It's different out on the shore where you get all that city riffraff. But, here . . . Why, Tom is supposed to do a weekly check on the summer places. Isn't he, Toddy? You know, Tom the state trooper, don't you, Mr. Bentwood? We just saw him last week, and he was saying how quiet it is in Flynders, what a relief it was to come to our little village. No crime around here. Right, boys? *I said, right?*"

Duane snickered and ground out his cigarette in his plate, instantly taking another. "Right, Daddy," said Warren.

"I'll go call Tom," Haynes said. "He's off today. Still, he

can just get his butt out there to your place. We'll take care of this situation."

"Did they steal any valuables?" asked Mrs. Haynes, looking at Sophie intently.

"Nothing seems to be missing," she answered. "They just wrecked what was there."

"It might be kids, you know," Mr. Haynes offered in a somewhat sorrowful voice, "after liquor. You summer people leave all that liquor around, you know. It's just too damn much for some young folks. You people come and go. But they have to stay. See what I mean? Right, boys?" He smiled and bent forward, a hand on each knee, his truculence gleaming through his smile like a stone under water. Mrs. Haynes absently tore off a piece of meat from the roast, which had cooled in its fat, and stuffed it into her mouth. Connie went back to her magazine.

"All right, folks. Let's go look at the damage," said Haynes. "Warren, when are you going to take that goddamn Caddie to the bone yard? I can't get the Chevy out of the shed with that thing lying there across the road."

"You can back it around like you always do," Warren snapped. "There's lots of things I want to take out of that wagon still. You said yourself this morning that there's a lot we can use in it."

Mr. Haynes shrugged helplessly. "Don't do a thing their father says," he told Otto. "No respect." And he smiled.

"We'll drive you back," Otto offered. "We'd like to get to it."

"Let me call Tom," said Haynes. He stood up and took a short leather jacket from a peg on the wall. "I haven't been out yet today. But it don't look cold. Is it?" Otto shook his head, then said "No" in a choked voice. Haynes left the room. Mrs. Haynes stared at the dirty dishes. Duane began to tap a glass with a spoon.

"Stop that noise!" cried Mrs. Haynes angrily. He gave her a fierce look and went to the back door, cursing it when the lock jammed, then yanking it open and slamming it behind him.

"We'll wait in the car," said Otto in Mrs. Haynes' direction. She nodded indifferently and then heaved a massive sigh. "Help me clear, Connie," she said. Connie shook her head, but her mother yanked her to her feet. As Sophie looked back, she saw mother and daughter laboriously removing dirty plates from the table.

"Tom'll meet us in half an hour," announced Mr. Haynes, fighting off the frantic embrace of Mamba as he got into the back seat of the Mercedes. He apologized elaborately for the dog as he shoved her out onto the ground, and then for his dirty boots. He seemed to suggest that the Bentwoods really would have preferred him to run along behind the car. Otto cut short his apologies by enumerating the damages to the house. When they drove into the yard, Sophie experienced an intense reluctance to go back into the house, but once inside, she felt a kind of lassitude.

Tom, the trooper, arrived in half an hour as he had promised. He was dressed nattily in civilian clothes, his hair was slicked down, his face clean-shaven, his expression bland and his voice impersonal.

"Could have been anyone," he said, after he had looked around. "There's been a lot of this kind of stuff these last few years. Kids, usually. They often don't take anything, maybe a radio or something little they can carry. Do you have a radio? No? And you can't find anything missing? Well, I don't suppose they'd have much use for what you've got in here." He waved his hand at the living room as though by his own estimate of the wreckage, there couldn't have been anything of much value.

"They're running wild these days," he said. "We got our hands full with drug takers, and the hippies from the city that hole up out here for the winter. One couple—you wouldn't believe it—they lived in someone's old barn for two months before we spotted them. They're not as dumb as they look, you know. These two knew our routine and when we came around to check up on the property, there wasn't a sign of life."

"No!" exclaimed Mr. Haynes. "You mean, a boy and a girl?"

"That's right," said Tom. "We might never have got them if they hadn't taken in some stray dog that set up a howl when we parked the car near the barn." Then he took care of official culpability by telling the Bentwoods he'd just been around to check on their house the week before. "Everything looked okay then," he said. "We didn't find any broken windows or anything." Sophie thought about the catbird. It had been dead a long time, and it wouldn't, in any case, have been flying around the house in dead winter. She glanced at Tom's impassive face. Perhaps he didn't even know he had lied; perhaps he only recognized a lie when it was refuted.

"But there is a dead bird in the tub," she said in a low, unsteady voice, "and it's been dead for a while."

Tom turned to Sophie and stared at her silently, his unblinking eyes fixed on hers. Then he said without emphasis, "We were out here last week."

"I'll go measure that window," said Mr. Haynes, "and get out here first thing in the morning to fix it. I think I got a piece of glass in the shed that ought to do." He took a round tape measure from his jacket pocket. "Look at that!" he cried happily. "I wasn't even sure it was going to be there when I reached in."

"What are we to do?" asked Otto. "Do we have to get bars for the windows?"

"I doubt they'll try again," Tom said, turning his back on Sophie. "I mean they've *taken* care of you. I'm sorry this happened. But at least, they didn't burn the house down. We've had two fires out at Mascuit."

"They burn up the whole house?" shouted Haynes from the bedroom. He walked back into the living room, trying to get the tape to roll back into its casing. "Damn thing's busted," he muttered.

"They burned both houses to the ground. One of the owners is in Europe and we can't even get hold of him." Sophie thought, or imagined, she heard a small note of satisfaction in Tom's voice. It was hard to tell; he didn't show much more than his bodily surface. God knows what was running around inside.

Tom departed with a belligerent shifting of gears, then Otto and Haynes got into the Mercedes and drove off.

Sophie ate half a ham sandwich and a hard-boiled egg in the kitchen, where there was less damage than in the other rooms.

Later, filling paper sacks with debris, she felt the beginning of composure. As she worked, she caught sight of the meadows through the kitchen window. The crumbling remains of an old stone wall caught the sunlight in its earth-filled crevices. She gathered up the dead bird in paper toweling and did what she could with the bathroom floor. There was no water to scrub it with. Then she found a shovel in the small basement and carried the pile of feces out behind the house and flung it as far as she could.

When Otto returned, she told him nothing had been taken except the flashlight she kept in their bedroom. And she was sure there had been very little bourbon left in the bottle she'd found beneath the table. He had gone to stand at the kitchen window and was looking out.

"What I'll miss most, after I'm dead," he said, "is that light in the late afternoon."

"They might have burned the house, Otto," she said. "It could have been much worse."

"I'll take out the bird and the crap," he said.

"I did that."

"It's a little like flushing the toilet just before the *Titanic* goes down," he said.

"We didn't sink," she said. "We've just been roughed up."

"I wish someone would tell me how I can live," he said, and shot her a glance. The half-question affected her unpleasantly, and she turned her head away instantly so he could not see her face. She felt the injustice of her own response—what if his words were puerile? The plea behind them was not. But *she* couldn't tell anyone how to live! Maybe it would have been all right if he hadn't looked at her—if he had cried out, forgetting self, forgetting how what he said might *sound*, if he had shouted, "I don't know how to live!"

"There's no one to say," she said flatly.

"Maybe we should move away."

"Where?"

"I can't even move away. I couldn't start up a practice at my age in Chicago, or any other place."

"I don't like Chicago."

"How about Halifax?"

"It's only furniture . . ."

"There isn't any place for the way I feel."

"Listen, Otto. *It was just furniture.*"

"But don't you see how savage it is? And empty . . . I wouldn't mind being shot in a revolution, or having my home burned. . . ."

She laughed wildly. "You wouldn't *mind* being shot!" she cried.

"There'd be some purpose to it," he said stubbornly, grabbing up a mutilated sketch of the house someone had drawn for them, and flourishing it at her. "*This* is meaningless. It doesn't represent an idea. It is primitive, the void . . ."

"Maybe it's in a language you don't speak—"

"Are you defending pigs who shit in your fireplace!" he demanded furiously.

"Oh, Otto," she said, and rested her head on her arm.

"I wonder if those Haynes cretins had something to do with it. How they hate us! Did you see how gratified they were by this trouble of ours? Everything in that kitchen was just the way they wanted it, Connie, and the television set on the washing machine, and Duane straddling his chair and that 1953 calendar—it all said one thing to me. It said, *die.*"

She went into the living room and looked around the bare walls. All the sweet, pretty things were gone, things she had found in junk shops or picked off the ground, or bought in antique stores. Otto took care of cars and insurance policies, real estate and hotel reservations, all that. But he was not a collector.

"I suppose we've got insurance to cover this," she called back to him.

"Give me a category," he said in a bitter voice, coming to the kitchen door, still holding the sketch. "What's it called?"

"Oh, Christ!" she exclaimed. "It's called vandalism, and that's all it's called. . . ."

They drove through the village without commenting on the familiar landmarks; the copper beeches looked dead, like stage trees, an affectation of value. Otto didn't stop for gas until they had reached the highway, departing from his custom of giving one of the Flynders stations his business.

The parkway drugged her. The car went up and down ramps like a mechanical toy at the end of a metal arm. It was midway to darkness; suddenly the lights came on. Then gradually, in the pale emptiness of her mind, there was a flush of memory. She had felt something like this once before, during the year after Francis had gone back to Locust Valley. Then, as now, a debilitating fatigue had overcome her. She had suffered slight but persistent fevers. Noel had shot her full of vitamin B-12 and bluntly suggested a consultation with a psychiatric colleague. She'd refused, coming out of her stupor long enough to say to Noel that as it was she couldn't bear to think about herself. She had lost weight, grown haggard, idle, and indifferent. She sat up violently, hitting her arm against the door. She didn't want that emptiness . . .

"What's the matter?" Otto asked.

"Nothing."

He spoke to her again, but she didn't understand him. He looked over at her. "I said, perhaps we'd better try to think about adopting a child again. Didn't you hear me?"

"All right."

"*All right!* Is that how you feel?"

"You've no right to ask me that. I exhausted feeling about that subject a long time ago. When I wanted to do it, you behaved as though I'd asked you to get me a harvester."

"Well, I'm thinking about it differently."

"I don't believe you're serious. If I thought you were serious . . ."

"Then what?"

"I don't know. . . ."

"Take my hand!" he demanded suddenly, and held his hand out toward her. She hesitated, then reached across herself with her right hand, and gripped his in it. He held it for a second.

"Is the bite still bothering you? I thought it was okay."

"It's still tender."

"Did you take those pills?"

"I forgot, out there."

"That's over, at least."

"Not yet. When will they kill the cat?"

They were going through Queens now, but in the dark, picked at feebly by the lights, it was only a series of roads.

"After they've examined it," he said.

"They don't keep it—well, I know it would be after they examined it, Otto. I mean, do they keep it for a week or a day or two, in case someone might take it?"

"That old brute? Who would take it?"

"Can you stay home tomorrow until noon?"

"Why do you persist in thinking they're going to call you?"

"There's always a chance they might."

"All right, then!" he exploded angrily. "Then you'll have the shots, fourteen of them, and they'll hurt, and possibly, they won't even work!"

She felt immensely cheered by his outburst.

"You don't understand," she said, almost gratefully. "It's what's behind it that bothers me."

"We've had a few bad days. There's nothing *behind* anything. What in God's name do you want? Do you want Charlie to murder me? Do you wish the farmhouse had been burned down? Do you wish that Negro man had killed us? And a bullet to have lodged itself in Mike Holstein's wall instead of a rock on the floor? *Do you want to be rabid?*"

"But, by extension, everything you say could have come true! One more step, one more minute—"

"But it didn't!" he shouted, driving jerkily and fumbling with the shift stick. "God, I went through a red light!"

"Can't you take the morning off?"

"No," he said harshly. "Especially not now."

"Especially now!"

"I *have* to be there. If I let go now, it'll be a disaster. Sophie—" he cried importunately, "it's all I know."

After a while, she said, "Never mind what I say."

"I can't," he replied quietly. "I don't and I can't."

She made supper for them while he went through his insurance file. After they'd eaten, they made a list of the repairs they would have to make, and what they'd have to replace. "All those beds," said Otto. "Why did they slash away so at those?" They'd have to let Haynes continue as caretaker. If they hired someone else, Haynes would do them in somehow.

"I noticed you hesitated to go in after I unlocked the door when we got home," Otto said.

"I had some morbid image," she said. "I thought they might have been here, too."

"Not yet," he said.

They read very late, sitting up in bed against pillows and drinking glasses of red wine. As usual, Otto fell asleep first.

The house creaked quietly to itself in the dark. Around three o'clock, an east wind blew down the street, moving the stiff young branches of the maple trees. A small gray mouse ran from beneath the Bentwood refrigerator, across the kitchen

floor, and out to the dining room, where it wedged itself beneath
an armoire in which Sophie kept the table linen.

It must have heard something that frightened it, for it
jammed itself still farther under the armoire, to a point where
the old cedar floor planking had buckled, then it could not back
out. The white-and-gray cat watched the telephone wires and
tree branches which the wind had stirred into movement. It
balanced itself with habitual ease on the narrow ledge of a fence
crosspiece. The man who lived in the house across the Bentwood
back yard, rose, stumbled to the window, and relieved himself.
The cat blinked and cocked its head, listening to the splatter of
water on the Victorian garden path. The man collapsed back
into bed. On the next floor, a small infant awoke and began to
cry. It cried for a long time by itself in the wet dark, its belly
and buttocks twisting and straining, the sheer force of its wails
lifting the small trunk up and down like a pump. The father
got up from his bed and crossed the room to the crib, where he
stood looking down into it. As his eyes grew accustomed to the
dark, he saw the vertical movement of the infant's body. He did
nothing; his hands hung at his sides, motionless. His T-shirt fell
to just below his navel, and he was conscious of the wind which
blew through cracks in the window, where the plastic had torn
loose from the tacks. The wind chilled his genitals and thighs,
and he curved his hands in front of himself, making a kind of
nest for his penis. He continued to observe his bawling son, holding his crotch in his hands. The baby often woke at this time of
morning, and the father would often come and observe him in
this way. He didn't know what his wife did, or thought, when it
was she who came to the crib. Tonight she had not stirred. All at
once, the child's wailing died away completely. A familiar odor
drifted up from the now relaxed and motionless body. "All that

for a shit!" the father muttered to himself in Spanish. "What a scandalous life it is. . . ."

The baby's cry had awakened Otto. He stared into the dark, listening to that distant squeal that was so like a cat's. By the time it suddenly stopped, he was thoroughly awake. He turned and saw the dark mass of Sophie's hair on the sheet beside him. She'd pushed the pillow off the bed in her sleep. He sniffed at her hair. There was a faint trace of the perfume she always wore, but it floated on a rather stronger chemical smell. That monstrous bottle he had given her had probably turned to alcohol. Next birthday, he would buy her three small bottles instead. He could tell by her breathing that her mouth was open against the sheet. He touched her hair. It was thick, strong, lively hair. The nape of her neck was warm, faintly damp where her hair was silkier, more tender somehow. He nestled his hand there, beneath the heavy mass; his hand seemed to be his whole self, hiding in the dark. She grumbled once, but he ignored her complaint. She was lying on her stomach. He grasped her shoulder and pulled her toward him until she sunk against him. He began to push up her short nylon gown. He knew she must be awake. But he would not speak her name. He would not say anything at all. Sometimes, over the years, that had happened, his not wanting to talk to her. It didn't mean he was angry. But sometimes, after a movie or a play or the company had gone home, he simply didn't want to talk to her. It was a very deep feeling, a law of his own nature that, now and then, had to be obeyed. He loved Sophie—he thought about her, the kind of woman she was—and she was so tangled in his life that the time he had sensed she wanted to go away from him had brought him more suffering than he had conceived it possible for him to feel.

He pressed his hand down flat on her hip. Still she said nothing. He was suddenly angry, but he realized, as he maintained his own stubborn silence, it was not because of sexual disappointment so much as an exasperation similar to what he felt when he had to grab her arm to make her keep up with him when they walked together down a street.

He tightened his grip on her hip and turned her toward him, and as she sank below him on her back he saw by a faint glimmer of street light shining through the cracks in the window shutters, the dark smudges of her closed eyes. Then, with no ceremony and perversely gratified by the discomfort he was inflicting on them both, he entered her. When he withdrew, after an orgasm of an intensity he had not expected, he had the fleeting thought that his sudden impulse had had little to do with sensuality.

She stirred slightly, then shifted to her side, drew up her legs and pushed her back up against him.

"Oh, well . . ." she murmured.

"Sorry," he whispered, then was choked by a wave of laughter.

He'd got her that time.

THIRTEEN

It was six in the morning. Through the open kitchen door, Sophie felt the morning sunlight on her bare feet like a sustained and mindless stare. She poured herself a shot glass of whisky, then drank it down hastily, catching glimpses, as her head fell back, of the waxed surface of kitchen cabinets, a flash of scoured pots, a line of sharp Sabatier knives gripped by a strip of magnet. She set the glass down in the sink and saw a line, like a slug's trail, of dried gray spume circling the drain, the residue, the mark of the night tides from a hidden urban sea of pipes and sewers. Turning on the tap, she flushed out the sink, making loud childish sounds of disgust, momentarily amused by her own noise. Then she walked quickly to the dining room, feeling a sudden intense desire for more sunlight, for signs of life in the windows across the yard.

A book lay open on the dining room table, a red pencil separating its pages. A cup stood next to it, and in the cup was a wilted slice of lemon. Otto must have come down to read during the night. Before or after he'd jumped her? she wondered, reminding herself she'd been maltreated but not feeling so.

The small still life echoing Otto's presence filled her with uncertainty. Although she had only just left him asleep upstairs, having waked in an instant from deep sleep to find herself standing next to the bed, shivering and displaced as though she'd spent the night illicitly, these reminders on the table, paradoxically, cast a doubt on his proximity. But then, it was probably the whisky. She had never had a drink at six in the morning—it was a hell of a way to start Monday.

He had underlined a passage and she bent over the book to read it. She caught a reference to antipopery riots, then: "Strings of boys of fourteen were hung up in a row to vindicate the law," and after that a quote from an observer: " 'I never saw boys cry so!' "

"To vindicate the law," had been underlined twice.

There was no end to it, she thought, looking through the door at the yard, not pausing in her mind to name the thing there was no end to. She closed the book on the pencil and put it away on a shelf, washed out the cup, and filled the coffee pot with water. As often as not, she slept late on Monday, but that tardiness continued to trouble her just as it had done in her childhood. She woke now, as she had then, to a faint malaise, a sense of a foothold gained just in time. Monday had always been a terrible trouble—once she had tried to stay awake all Sunday night to forestall her mother's grim and unforgiving presence in her doorway—but she had fallen asleep just before dawn, to be awakened two hours later by her mother clapping her hands relentlessly over the bed, her face shining from her morning scrub, dressed in a starched house dress, saying over and over, "Early risers are the winners." It had been thirty years since Sophie had been roused by that derisive applause; she had not yet discovered the nature of the prize her mother's words had once led her to believe existed. Perhaps winning had simply meant the tyranny of waking others.

A man across the way was watching her. She stared back through the quiet sunny space between them, not aware that she was really looking at him, until she saw his grin, saw the T-shirt that ended just below his navel, saw his hands that had been clasped before his loins slowly part. She turned away quickly, thinking, that is *his* prize. Then, sneaking another look back, saw that he was now holding an infant in his arms, kissing its neck with an intensity she could almost feel on her own.

In her mother's house, blessings had been enumerated every day, a joyless catechism in which (her father having abjured all recitation) she had had to take part, if only with a ritual *"yes"* as her mother shouted, "You have space, good food, new shoes, a room of your own, toys, clean clothes, education, background . . ." While small Sophie nervously ate raisins and cried, *"Yes, yes, yes. . . ."* On a Sunday now and then, the three of them got into the Buick at her mother's insistence, and drove to where "the poor people" lived. It was the tail-end of the Depression, but in those streets they traveled the Depression could not end. Sophie's mother had driven the car with thick-skinned efficiency, her head locked into position like a piece of ordnance, eyes straight ahead, triumphant in her silence. When she said poor people, she *meant* poor people.

How had Otto felt, reading those lines sometime during the night? Had the hanging of young boys appalled him? But why had he underlined the words? Did he mean that the horror of law is that it must be vindicated? Or had he thought of himself, of his own longing for order? Or was the double line an expression of irony? Or did he think law was only another *form* of that same brute impulse which it was directed toward restraining? They had been married for fifteen years. What did she know of what he thought? She knew him in the density of their life together, not outside of it.

"What are you doing up so early?"

"Drinking," she answered. Otto yawned, then caught sight of the whisky bottle in her hand.

"Oh! You really are . . ."

"It's very good in the morning," she said. "Much better than at parties."

"Let's see your hand."

She held it out for his inspection. "The swelling has gone completely, hasn't it . . . doesn't look bad at all," he said.

"You look as if you'd been on a binge," she said. "Were you up all night?" She began to set the table for breakfast.

"For a while. I read and had some tea. Then I went back to sleep, then the baby woke me. . . . You're not worried about the tests on the cat now, are you? I've never seen you up so early, not since we were first married."

"Did I used to get up before you?" she asked, surprised, as though he had given her startling news that had some immediate relevance.

He was pouring himself coffee.

"Are you? Are you still worried?" he asked, apparently forgetting what she had asked him.

"Until I hear from them, I probably will be."

"But they won't call, Sophie."

"What a nasty indifferent way to manage things! I have to

wait until noon without a word from them. Then, a minute later, I'm supposed to know everything is all right?"

"I can't stand that frozen orange juice—"

"What law has to be vindicated?" she asked.

He rubbed his face vigorously with both hands as he always did in the mornings before he shaved, and have her a puzzled look.

"What law?"

"A sentence you underlined in that book you were reading. I found it here on the table with your red pencil."

He looked at her reflectively, then set down the can of orange juice he had started to open. "It is never vindicated," he said at last. "The law is a process, not an absolute. It'll take my whole life to understand it."

"Those hanged children were absolutes," she said bitterly. Then she added, her voice spiteful, "That's one thing I know about the difference between you and Charlie. He's not going to spend his days meditating on the nature of the law!" What in God's name had she said? She'd been so intensely angry, but what she'd said—well, she'd meant something cataclysmic, crushing, final. Instead, she'd come out with some gibberish.

"You're right about that," Otto said flatly. "Charlie is not going to *think* about anything. I was considering sending him a telegram—to his new quarters. I was going to say: 'Congratulations on a successful life!' " He gave her a cold, sad look, then trudged down the hall, but returned shortly with the daily newspaper in his hand.

"Do you think I would have had those children hanged?" he asked her.

"I don't know," she said.

"I don't even know how I would have felt. It would, I suppose, have depended upon whether I was a Catholic or a Protestant in 1790."

She groaned aloud, then slammed down the butter dish. The hatred she felt toward him was so unexpected, so powerful, she felt as though she'd hurled herself across the table at him. He walked quickly to her and put his hand on her arm.

"Sophie . . ." he said softly. "I couldn't hang a cat. . . . What is it? What is it?"

"I'll get dressed," she murmured, turning away her Medusa's face, feeling herself disfigured by the detestation that had so quickly possessed her and was now, just as quickly, draining away.

At breakfast, they avoided each other's glance. They read the newspaper, exchanging sections without comment.

Just as he was about to leave, Sophie asked him if he thought Charlie would be in the office today. He hoped not, he replied. Charlie had had all the time anyone would need to clean things up. No one was giving anyone a party. "It's the way things really end," he said.

"I wish you could stay home," she said despondently.

"I would . . . if it were really necessary."

"Necessary!"

He grabbed up his briefcase, gave her a look of pure exasperation, and shouted, "Sophie! It's too much!" and closed the door on whatever she might have shouted back.

It was eight thirty.

She was indignant that he had gone, leaving her in the chilly entryway, still wordlessly begging that some incident would force him back, that he would have forgotten something, and that once he opened the door, he would not see any reason for going. She even waited several minutes, poised forward, listening. He was like everyone else, witlessly inflexible, treating his own actions as if they stemmed from inexorable natural laws. Damn him! He had closed her *out* into the house!

But how ridiculous it would have been had he stayed! Both of them, brooding about the house, waiting for the telephone to ring ... Madam, the cat was rabid ... go to the Board of Health.

Was it the phone call she was afraid of? Or was it that she knew she would refuse those inoculations? Was that why, against all reason, reassurances, statistics, she continued to believe in nothing but the event itself? And that the appalling certainty that the phone would ring before noon did not arise from reason or its systems, but was a fatal estimate of her true life?

"God, if I am rabid, I am equal to what is outside," she said out loud, and felt an extraordinary relief as though, at last, she'd discovered what it was that could create a balance between the quiet, rather vacant progression of the days she spent in this house, and those portents that lit up the dark at the edge of her own existence.

She cleaned up the kitchen, saying to herself over and over, I have to think.

Think, she commanded her reflection in the bathroom mirror. Then she covered her face with a cream that had cost $25 for four ounces. She observed the terrible and irreversible vigor of the white hairs that thrust their coarse way among the black hairs. Her mouth was softening, spreading into ambiguity; the sharp outline of her chin was being erased by a subtle pouching of the flesh. She wiped off the cream and washed her face roughly with soap. When she looked back once more into the mirror, cleansed, her cheeks and forehead naked as a body can be naked, she smiled winningly, hoping to forestall some judgment against herself that she felt forming in the wake of her investigation of her fading surface. But the judgment—whatever it had been—slipped away before she could grasp it.

What she saw, for an instant, were her father's defeated energies in her eyes, and mixed with that, the insistent force of her mother's lineaments, all transformed mysteriously into herself. She touched the glass, finger on glass finger.

The phone rang. She went to it without haste. She wasn't expecting anything now.

It was Tanya, the spinster Sophie had known for years, who telephoned her from time to time. She must have broken off with a man or started up with a new one. They rarely saw each other now, although once there had existed between them a tie of sorts, one of sensibility perhaps. That had been when Sophie was still caught up with translations, and in the way of her work had met a number of people who had at the time seemed interesting to her. Tanya was the only one she continued to hear from. She had worked then, and still did, for a French news agency, and had once written a short essay on *Adolphe* which had been published by a three-pound quarterly, which had disappeared after the fifth issue, dead of its own weight perhaps. Despite the essay's eccentric and precious style, Sophie had been struck by its vigor, such a *hot* vigor in comparison to Tanya's cold, thin, aging-girl personality. She was home today, recovering from a cold, and had suddenly thought of Sophie, she said, wondered how she was, if she was working on anything, they hadn't seen each other in so long, and did Sophie think she ought to go to Peru or Mexico this summer? But before Sophie could answer, Tanya went on to describe the latest in her staggeringly long succession of affairs.

Sophie sat down heavily on the bed, gripping the phone and staring fixedly at the hands of the clock on her bedside table.

There had been so many men for Tanya—she was like a time capsule into which men deposited messages that were to be read in the dust centuries hence. No man had ever, apparently, reached that mother's girl. She remained, as always, a birdlike voice on the phone, dressed at the moment for convalescence, Sophie was sure, in an expensive and ill-fitting housecoat, implacable, imperturbable, grossly virginal. She's mad, thought Sophie. She's not a whore, she's not frigid—just a lunatic.

"His wife is a clod," said Tanya. "The poor little animal crawls into my bed as if it were Chartres. Do you know, he's painted my whole flat for me! Three coats! He's got arthritis of the wrist, too, but he knows how broke I am and the walls were that New York *despair* color, so he just did it himself. He's a darling little animal—"

"Why don't you make a retreat for six months!" Sophie interrupted, shouting. "Don't you know how *dumb* you are? You think because somebody's husband sticks it in you, that you've *won!* You poor dumb old collapsed bag! *Who are you kidding!*"

God, had she killed her dead? There wasn't a sound at the other end of the telephone, not a whisper of breath. Sophie was trembling, her hands wet. Then she heard a kind of hiss that became words, spilling liquidly, like broken teeth from a hurt mouth.

"You . . . filthy . . . cunt!" it said. Sophie dropped the phone on its hook.

She began to clean the house scrupulously, averting her mind from the astonishing exchange that had taken place on the phone, and from her own furious outburst, giving her whole attention now to the lavender-scented English wax with which she was polishing the furniture.

The peak hour of morning traffic had passed. It was quiet

outside on the street. But that was a deception. There was a siege going on: it had been going on for a long time, but the besieged themselves were the last to take it seriously. Hosing vomit off the sidewalk was only a temporary measure, like a good intention. The lines were tightening—Mike Holstein had known that, standing in his bedroom with the stone in his hand—but it was almost impossible to know where the lines were.

Sophie made herself a cup of strong coffee and went to her desk in the bedroom. She must write to her mother before the urge died, before it was too late. She would have something to tell her this time, a story to cover the emptiness of the page, to belie the true silence between them which had begun when Sophie had left home, after she had awakened for the last time to that jeering applause. She would write her about the cat; her mother would enjoy that. She would describe the incident in such a way it would strike the exact note calculated to arouse the old woman's scorn and hilarity.

From a drawer she took out paper and envelope. She filled the old fountain pen Otto had found for her in an antique shop from a small crystal ink bottle that stood on its own silver claw feet. The foot of the desk chair was caught in the fringes of the rug and, just as she bent down to disentangle it, she heard the sound of a key in the front door. She stood up and glanced at the bedside clock in surprise. It was a few minutes before noon. Otto's footsteps were audible on the stairs; then he walked into the bedroom.

"I took care of a few things, then planned to come right home," he said. He looked very tired. "I was going to call you to tell you I was coming, but I was afraid the phone's ringing would scare you. You'd think it was about the cat turning up crazy. The subway was awful. I was wild . . . I left the office at ten thirty and it's taken me all this time. Some youths were on a rampage. They broke some windows and . . . *youths!*" With consuming bitterness, he repeated the last word. "So the trains were all delayed. I didn't know what to do."

"It was all right," she said. "The A.S.P.C.A. didn't call, of course. I suppose they'll get rid of the cat right away? What do they do? Garrote it? But someone did phone. Tanya. It started out to be our usual conversation. Then I dropped the other shoe. I mean, I told her I was sick of her. She called me a filthy cunt."

Otto winced. He didn't like that. Sophie laughed. "Oh, it was the correct adjective, *filthy*, the one she really meant to use. She is like a *fairy*, you know. Stop looking that way! I felt bad, but only for a second."

"What have you been doing since I left?"

"Not much. Just now, I thought I'd write to my mother. I thought of something to tell her about." He was staring at her.

"I'm glad you came home," she said.

The extension phone on the desk rang. With a certain reluctance, he reached for it. She shook her head and placed her hand on the receiver. "I *know* they won't call now. I tell you, I know it," she said irritably. She picked up the phone.

"Sophie? Is Otto there?" asked Charlie Russel. "I called the office and they said he'd left to go home. I have to talk to him."

"Just a minute." She held the phone out to Otto. "It's Charlie." Otto shook himself like a wet dog. "No! No! I won't talk to him."

"He won't talk to you," Sophie repeated into the mouthpiece.

"I've *got* to talk to him," Charlie cried. "There are a thousand things . . . how long does he think he can avoid this? What about precedent contracts? *You put him on!*" She held out the receiver again. Otto looked down at it. They could both hear Charlie's diminished voice like an insect cry.

"I'm desperate!" screeched the round black hole.

"*He's* desperate!" Otto shouted. His distraught glance suddenly fell upon the ink bottle on Sophie's desk. His arm shot out and he grabbed it up and flung it violently at the wall. Sophie dropped the phone on the floor and ran to him. She flung her arms around him so tightly that for a moment he could not move.

The voice from the telephone went on and on like gas leaking from a pipe. Sophie and Otto had ceased to listen. Her arms fell away from his shoulders as they both turned slowly toward the wall, turned until they could both see the ink running down to the floor in black lines.

Don't miss other titles by
PAULA FOX

"Vividly rendered. . . . Haunting
. . . [Fox] writes with silken ease
and a sensitivity to nuance."
—*Newsday*

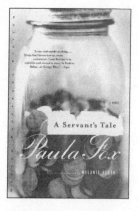

"A rare and wondrous thing.
. . . [Fox] knows how to create a
character."
—*Vogue*

"Chekhovian. . . . Every line of
Fox's story, every gesture of her
characters, is alive and surprising."
—Christopher Lehmann-Haupt,
New York Times

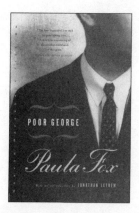

"The best first novel I've read in
quite a long time."
—Bernard Bergonzi,
New York Review of Books